THE LONELY RIDE

THE LONELY RIDE

GILES A. LUTZ

DOUBLEDAY & COMPANY, INC.

GARDEN CITY, NEW YORK

1971

THE LONELY RIDE

CHAPTER ONE

The column of men and horses seemed lost in the vast reaches of the emptiness of Wyoming. This country promised nothing easy, and it showed in the past, tortured upheaval of the mountains that bit at the sky with long, jagged jaws. The same lack of promise was in the great bowl of the sky that could blister a man with its sun even while the savage winds gathered new strength to freeze him. Just existing in it was a chore, and these men showed the demands it had made upon them. They rode slack-shouldered with a complete inattention to the dangerous country they were going through. The horses were as jaded, and it showed in their heavy hoofs.

Captain William J. Fetterman stood in the stirrups to make a sweeping search of the country, winding up with an appraisal of the men behind him. Their heads drooped, and their eyes were half-closed. Reins were loose in limp fingers, and men were sunk deep in somnolence. If the horses were startled into a sudden jump or bolt, half of the column would be dumped on the ground.

"Sergeant," Fetterman bawled. His voice crackled with anger. "Tighten up that column." It was straggling again.

"Yes, sir." Sergeant Murphy's chin snapped up from his chest, and his beefy face flushed with resentment at the criticism in Fetterman's order.

"You heard the captain," he roared. "Tighten up, tighten up. Or do I have to break your heads to get something into them?"

1

The heavy timbre of his voice beat at the men, and it showed in the stiffening of their faces. They dared make no audible protest. This was Murphy's privilege. In the Army a man passed on his resentment to lesser rank, and the troopers had no one below them.

Fetterman watched heads raise and shoulders snap back. At least, they looked more like Army.

He sank back into his saddle, the grimace of disapproval still molding his face. "I hope our scouts are showing more alertness. My God, they were half-asleep in their saddles."

"It's beginning to catch up with them, sir."

Fetterman flashed a look at the man riding beside him. He wanted to demand just what Lieutenant Thomas Hutson meant by that, but he knew. That was criticism of his forcing the march ever since they left Fort Laramie. All right! He had forced it, but he would be damned, if he needed an excuse for it. Hadn't Fort Phil Kearny asked for reinforcements? An officer didn't dawdle on a mission like that. The cynical smile reshaped his lips. He had cut better than a day off of the usual travel time from Laramie to Kearny. He didn't give a damn what Hutson thought about it; he considered it an accomplishment.

"Do you think I'm pushing them too hard, Mr. Hutson?"

Hutson was wise enough not to voice his personal opinion, particularly if it conflicted with higher authority. That lesson was taught early at West Point.

"No, sir. Not if you don't think so."

"You don't think Kearny needs the reinforcements?"

Hutson's face was blank, as he picked out his answer. "I don't know, sir. Colonel Carrington didn't seem to when he passed Laramie." He didn't know what Carrington had run into, or what had been in his reports.

Fetterman gave him grudging approval. Hutson was young, but he had a clever head on his shoulders. He wasn't going to say anything that could slam back at him. It was common knowledge that General Philip St. George Cooke, in Omaha, was anything but satisfied with Carrington's handling of the

Sioux problem. Colonel Henry B. Carrington sat behind his walls at Fort Phil Kearny and let Indian raid after raid on the emigrant trains go unpunished. The last Carrington report that drove Cooke wild was that he considered the Bozeman Trail to be unsafe, and that he was closing it. Fetterman could imagine the explosion that rocked Cooke's office when he received that. When Cooke was dissatisfied, he loped off heads. Fetterman had heard no official word, but he was satisfied that he was being sent to Kearny to replace Carrington. That was the urgency behind the march. He wanted to get to Kearny as fast as he could for personal reasons.

"Do you think the Sioux are dangerous?" He made no attempt to veil the sneer in his voice.

"Yes, sir." That was no hesitancy in Hutson's answer. Fetterman's laugh had a jarring note. "I find that hard to believe, Mr. Hutson, if they're all like those I saw around Laramie."

"They're not, sir. We called those Sioux the Laramie loafers. They hung around, begging for any handout they could get. Those were the tired, old men of the Sioux nation. The treaty commission talked to them and went away convinced the Sioux want only peace."

"You think there are other kind?" The sneer was open on Fetterman's face.

"I do, sir. The young hotheads rode away with Red Cloud. But before he left he saw Colonel Carrington and his command." His voice had a new, peculiar flatness.

Hutson inferred that the meeting between Carrington and Red Cloud had particular meaning. Fetterman didn't know what it was. "What was bad about that?"

"Colonel Carrington was sent out to build Fort Reno and Fort Phil Kearny."

Fetterman waited for further explanation, and it didn't come. He showed his annoyance. Hutson had a trick of putting out a statement that needed explanation, then letting it dangle. Was Hutson saying that the meeting between Car-

3

rington and Red Cloud was the basis of this recent Indian outbreak? He almost snorted at the ridiculous question.

"Are you saying that Red Cloud resented Colonel Carrington being sent out here to build those forts?"

For a moment, it looked as though Hutson regretted going this far. "Sir, I'm only saying what some of the old Indian heads said. We promised Red Cloud that we would not violate his last hunting ground. Then gold was found in the Black Hills."

Fetterman choked back an oath. The politics of a matter never concerned him. He did the job that was handed him and wasn't bothered about anything else.

"Go on," he snapped.

"Gold meant more settlers pouring up the Bozeman Trail. Carrington's mission was to build more forts to give additional protection to the trail."

Fetterman frowned at him. Hutson sounded as though he was against that policy. It wasn't his place to be for or against it. Congress set the policy, and the Army carried it out. Fetterman saw nothing to be upset about because some Indian disagreed with Congress.

His laugh was brittle. "Are you saying that Red Cloud made up his mind that no more forts would be built?"

"Yes, sir. The Black Hills are the last hunting ground of the Sioux, Captain. The more white settlers pour into it the greater becomes the threat to the game. Red Cloud looks ahead and sees nothing left for his people. It frightens him into fighting."

Hutson nettled Fetterman. He had heard talk like this before but always from outside of the Army. It was a rare trend of thought to find in the Army, particularly in the officer ranks.

He glowered at Hutson from under lowered brows. "You sound like you feel as Red Cloud does."

Hutson promptly denied it. "No, sir. I was just thinking of the price it's going to cost. The Sioux are gathering around Red Cloud. It's a big and powerful nation."

4

Fetterman could feel the heat of the blood flowing into his face. Hutson's last statement convinced him of one thing; Hutson had a glaring weakness in him. Hadn't he jumped to the troopers' defense because he thought they were tired? Fetterman almost snorted. Hutson's attitude was an example of what was wrong with the Army. Too many officers compared the objective with the human cost in accomplishing it. Thank God, such an outlook hadn't muddied his thinking.

He turned in the saddle for another look behind him. The men rode smartly enough now. He thought sardonically that they had been stung because of his order to Sergeant Murphy, and it caused him not the slightest concern. He understood everything about the incident. Hutson thought his defense of the men was reasonable. Hadn't he been over them at Laramie? Reasonable to him, Fetterman thought; not to me.

This was another weakness he had discovered in Hutson. Because the lieutenant was familiar with the men, he let it weaken his authority. Too many junior officers made that mistake. If Fetterman had had any tendency toward that mistake, he had eliminated it early in his career.

He studied Hutson's profile, half-expecting to see dislike of him in the face. He saw no thinning in the lips, nor a tightening in the cheeks. It might have disappointed him a little for he was quite prepared to rake him for the feeling. He admitted that for a man so young Hutson had excellent control of his feelings.

He rode in silence, picking through his words, wanting the exact ones to let Hutson know what he thought of such adolescent thinking.

He glanced again at Hutson. Hutson was aware of it, but he stared straight ahead. Every year, they came out of the Point younger, Fetterman thought. He mulled over what Hutson said, and it lodged in his throat. It showed a mawkish sentimentality, and it poorly fitted an officer. Was this Hutson's thinking? Fetterman pondered over the point. He doubted it. Hutson was too young for such thoughts to be his

5

own. He had talked to somebody, and Fetterman wanted to know who that man was.

He did not like Hutson, and he would not consider it a snap judgment. He didn't need long to be able to make up his mind about a man. Let him talk to a man for only a few minutes, and he could determine whether or not the man was worth liking.

He looked again at Hutson. His mind is a garbage pail, he thought dourly. It is entirely receptive to anything anybody wanted to throw into it.

The afternoon sun picked up the golden fuzz on Hutson's jawline. If he had packed a razor in his possessions, Fetterman would say that it would see rare use.

He prided himself upon being a fair man, and the fuzz wasn't enough on which to base a dislike. Hutson's enthusiasm could be a part of that dislike. Fetterman nodded. That might be it. He had been around that eager, bubbling enthusiasm to have it grate on his nerves. A couple of times he had sat on it hard, but that hadn't abashed Hutson. All he would do was grin, then come up with another plan. It was more than enough to sour an older man.

Hutson's face was well-hewn, and the blue eyes were that light shade that could be so penetrating. He was set up well in the shoulders and chest, but it wasn't the physical aspect of him that irked Fetterman. It was his thinking, and the gorge over it was still lodged in Fetterman's throat.

He had scathing words with which to cut Hutson down, but before he delivered them he wanted more information. "Is this your thinking, Mr. Hutson, or did somebody pump you full?"

Hutson caught the jeering note in the question for he flushed. "I talked to everybody I could, sir. Everybody whom I thought would know about it. Members of the treaty commission, the famous scouts, Jim Bridger and Portugee Phillips—" He let the words fade away, remembering the wide gap between the thinking he had listened to. He had stumbled through opposite viewpoints, trying to find the truth

6

from the self-servicing words. He had spent troubled hours measuring one against the other, and logic lay with the men who really knew the Indian and his problem. He had a shy, half-grin on his face. "I wish you could have talked to them too, sir."

Fetterman said an oath that brought the color back into Hutson's face. He knew Bridger and Phillips only by hearsay, and he had no desire to know them further.

"Professional scouts," he said. "A small cut above the Indian. They take the dollars the Army hands them, but where is their true allegiance?"

Hutson opened his mouth, then slowly closed it.

It gave Fetterman harsh amusement. He had no doubt that Hutson wanted to spring to the defense of Bridger and Phillips, then had thought better of it.

"They are nothing but squaw men, Mr. Hutson. They live with the Indians and produce half-breeds that will only increase our problem. They live among them so much they think more like an Indian than an Indian does."

Hutson's face was getting that flinty look. "You're wrong, sir. At least about Phillips. I met his wife and two children. They're as white as you and I are."

"That's enough," Fetterman snapped. He had gone out on queasy ground with that part of his statement about Bridger and Phillips being squaw men. Hutson was ready to argue about it, bolstered by his conviction that he knew what he was talking about. Fetterman was sorry that he had given Hutson this advantage.

They rode in stony silence, the dislike between them flowing in almost tangible waves. Fetterman was certain of one thing; if Hutson was assigned to his command after they reached Phil Kearny, he would do a lot of remaking of the man.

He was a tall, supple man, fitting superbly into a saddle. He gave with every movement of the horse, and there was no lack of communication between rider and animal. His hair was jet-black, and up to a short time ago, he had worn a full

7

beard, proud of its wiry crispness. When he had decided to eliminate the beard, he had let the mustache remain, and it was full and flowing. In moments of deep thought, he had the habit of pulling on it. He would be the first to deny that it was due to vanity, but he liked the wiry feeling of it. He knew his capacities, and the knowledge was fuel to the smoldering fire of impatience within him.

He put another look behind him and saw nothing for additional criticism. He smiled thinly. Every head was up, and the mask of faces hid the disapproval of him. He wasn't popular with enlisted men, but few officers built a record on that foundation. His record apologized to no one. He had been a brevet lieutenant colonel in the Civil War, and for his personal ambition, that war had ended too soon. There was no telling of how far he could have gone, if the war had lasted another year. He had been trained at West Point in the art of eliminating an enemy, and it was only in war times that he could practice his skill. An officer fared poorly during the years of peace. A man stagnated in them, and the promotions came few and far between. He had been knocked back to the rank of captain and thinking of the torturous climbing back had galled his soul. He was quite happy about this so-called war with the Sioux. It couldn't last very long, but an aggressive officer could make capital of it.

He knew exactly what he wanted to say, and he made no effort to soften it. "Mr. Hutson, do you know what I think of your Sioux nation? Give me eighty men, and I could cut straight through the heart of it."

The shocked disbelief in Hutson's face tickled him. "You and Colonel Carrington should get along very well. You think alike."

Before Hutson could answer that the faint popping of rifle fire turned their heads. Fetterman swore to himself. He hadn't told the scouts to get that far ahead.

He stood in the stirrups and waved his arm forward. All of his sourness dropped away from him. He was living again.

8

CHAPTER TWO

Two troopers burst out of the brush and raced toward them. They quirted their horses, and the riders were as savagely lashed by panic. Their haste screamed urgency, and Fetterman frowned. Not at their need of haste but at the fact he had sent out three scouts, and only two were coming back.

"Keep your place," he barked to Hutson and galloped ahead to meet the two men.

Brashear and Linn were white-faced and wild-eyed. Their lips were strained back from their teeth as they gulped for breath, and Fetterman felt no tolerance for their panic.

They pulled to a skidding stop, and there was no refuge in Fetterman's cold survey.

"Well?" The voice and eyes matched.

"Indians, sir," Brashear gasped. He was a short, stocky man with a soft fold of flesh covering his jowls. In an Army uniform he looked as far out of place as a man could be. Fetterman knew his record. The man was not battle-tested. The Army had far too many such men.

"You ran from them?" Fetterman sounded as though he tasted something bad.

"They were all around us, sir," Linn protested. He had the lanky build and movement of a countryman, and Fetterman doubted that the Army would ever find the uniform to fit him.

The two came out of different environments, but in Fetterman's opinion they were cast in the same mold. He had too

9

often seen their type in the Army, and it always aroused a flame of anger in him.

"You ran off and left Jennings?" His contempt for them was in voice and eye.

"They cut him down on the first volley, sir." Brashear's voice climbed and threatened to buckle. "We couldn't do anything for him. We were lucky to get out, ourselves."

Fetterman let the silence grow until its weight was a crushing burden.

Linn tried to ease it. "They jumped us. We didn't know they were anywhere around."

The flame of anger grew until it seared Fetterman. This was what he had sent out as scouts, and they hadn't the slightest suspicion that Indians were near. They had been surprised, then ran without the slightest attempt to bring back Jennings. Fetterman doubted they had stopped to check whether or not Jennings was alive. Dead by now, he thought bleakly. The Indians had all the time they needed to finish their work. By God, he would see that these two regretted that.

He stared at them with a cold and bitter dislike. He didn't feel the loss of Jennings. He doubted that he could even describe the man. These two had not fulfilled their responsibility, and Fetterman had the certainty that it was the result of carelessness. Fatigue and perhaps boredom had dulled their eyes. They would deny it, but whatever was the cause Fetterman would not accept it as an excuse.

"How many Indians were there?"

They looked at each other, and Fetterman correctly read it. Eyes sent a helpless appeal to eyes that didn't know.

Disgust washed over Fetterman's face. He waited for an answer that he could rip apart.

He smelled the rancidity of men who hadn't washed for far too long. Fear was the major part of that, for this was November, and neither sun nor the exertion had been enough to raise a sweat that sent out its aroma. The odor of leather and the heated reek of horse flesh blended into a familiar smell. At least, the horses had earned their right to smell like this. Probably only a small body of Indians was involved. His scouts had stumbled upon them, and he wondered if they had stayed long enough to return fire. He could check their carbines, but he didn't have to. The terror in their eyes was answer enough. His big regret was that the Indians had fled before he could get the column there.

"Well?" he demanded.

"Hundreds, sir." Brashear looked at Linn in an agony of fear that he would dispute it.

Linn's gulp bobbed his Adam's apple. "That's right, sir."

"We'll see." Fetterman's tone promised they would regret it, if the information was wrong.

He whipped around and galloped back. He raved at himself for sending these men, but he doubted there was any better material in the column. After the Civil War, the Army had become nothing but a heaven for the beaten, men whom the failures of life had hammered into nonentities. He thought of the men he had commanded in the last year of the war. Those men had been seasoned veterans, men who had taken orders and carried them out without question or hesitation. What he could do with them now. But most of the veterans had mustered out of the Army after the war. Brashear and Linn were prime examples of what was given to an officer. Their inefficiency was a deep fog, wrapping around a man until he wanted to scream at its shrouding.

He discarded the first plan that came into his mind. He could prepare a position here and wait for an attack. But that would be a passive defense, and he detested it. It was alien to his nature. Throwing back an enemy wasn't enough when he wanted to smash it. His eyes gleamed as he considered cutting clear through them, clear to the gate of Kearny, if necessary. What better arrival could he want?

He ordered out a line of pickets and held a brief conference with his six officers; five misters and a captain re-

11

cently promoted. All green, he thought, with the common trouble of a lack of experience. Battle-tested was his one criterion of an officer or enlisted man.

His eyes were agate-hard. They sat straight-backed enough, and they were lean and hard in the flanks. That could be learned at the Point, and he gave it little consideration. The innards of them wouldn't be known until bullets did their probing.

"Brashear and Linn report Indians." He watched for their reaction. "They claim hundreds are up the trail."

He saw a tightening of cheek and a thinning of lips, but he could give them credit that no eyes wavered.

"You don't believe that report, sir?"

Fetterman gave Hutson a grudging approval. Hutson had a keen perceptiveness for what lay behind a tone.

"I do not. They ran into a band of Indians, all right. Jennings was killed. Brashear and Linn didn't wait long enough to evaluate anything." He snorted with a return of his disgust.

"Are we going ahead, sir?"

Experience might hammer Hutson into an acceptable officer, if that eagerness could be curbed and turned in the right direction.

"We are." Fetterman cast about in his mind, wishing he knew the Indian thinking. Had they fled, waited, or were sneaking up on them? Whichever it was, his plan could be changed as conditions changed. He hoped they had waited. He wanted to hack them to pieces. He would carry that to Carrington. Eventually, it had to filter back to Cooke.

He made his decision without a lingering qualm, accepting the fact they could be outnumbered without its rasping worry.

"Mr. Hutson, take a dozen men and proceed until you make contact. Then dismount and hold your position until we reach you." He smiled with malicious satisfaction at the startled flash in Hutson's eyes. "If that alarms you, I will assign another officer."

12

Its implication put a dull flush in Hutson's face. "I will take them, sir."

"To ease your concern, we'll move forward at the sound of engagement. I hope you can keep them occupied until I can slash through them." He knew that familiar, enjoyable tingle along his spine. He had never fought an Indian, but he knew the awesome power of a determined cavalry charge. Cold steel could put a flinching in the most seasoned troops. Those savages couldn't begin to stand against it.

He watched Hutson put his detail into a forager's line. Hutson displayed the outward signs of his trade, but West Point taught that on the parade grounds. But the Point couldn't determine the depths of a man. That would have to be discovered in the field.

Fetterman called Sergeant Murphy and two other noncoms to him.

"Indians, sir?" No upset was in Murphy's voice. He had a ponderous chest, his legs trimmed by long hours in the saddle. He was an old and seasoned campaigner, and he was rarely disturbed. His eyes were hooded in a heavy face, and they seldom missed anything.

Fetterman smiled sourly at him. "A guess, Sergeant?"

"No, sir. I saw the way Brashear and Linn come back. Without Jennings."

Fetterman saw the quick start of alarm in the other noncommissioned officers. Murphy would hold them in line.

"Pick four of your best men, Sergeant. Send them ahead of the main body until they hear engagement. At the first sound of Mr. Hutson's contact with the Sioux we will be in full saber charge."

He looked sharply at Murphy. Was that a flicker of distrust in those flinty eyes? If so, it was gone before he could be sure.

"Yes, sir." Murphy wheeled his horse and moved back to the troopers.

Fetterman watched him go along the line and issue the captain's orders. He could rely on Murphy and perhaps a few of the others. What the remainder did depended upon stronger wills, holding them in check.

Troopers drew sabers, and using their neckerchiefs, tied the hilts to their wrists. It could save a cavalryman from losing his weapon. A saber could be wrenched from a hand by jamming against bone after cutting through yielding flesh.

The flicker in Murphy's eyes still rankled Fetterman. Normal enough, he conceded. Trust flowed both ways between an enlisted man and officer but only after long, shared experience. He didn't know Murphy well enough to make a final judgment. Murphy did the proper things now, but that came from the habit of long routine. Fetterman would know him better this afternoon.

He looked ahead at the scouts, and they were spread in a widely spaced line. He had caught the unease in their faces as they cantered by. They would be alert enough, he thought dourly.

The tension crept along his muscles until he felt their stiff reply. But that would disappear at the first action. He pushed ahead in a slow trot, knowing his first contentment in several months. He had never been cut out to be a barrack soldier.

He hadn't ridden a half mile when he heard the first shot, thin and reedy because of the distance. Other shots came on the heels of the echo of the first one. He would say it was controlled fire, and if so, it would be Hutson's.

He hadn't seemed to draw a half-dozen breaths, when his scouts crashed back toward him. They hadn't waited for anything. He had hoped they would have crept forward to learn where the action was, and how many Indians were involved in it. He would have to go ahead on his own judgment, but he had already decided upon that.

He let them pound by him without an attempt to halt them. The frozen mask of his face wasn't conducive to make them want to talk to him.

He stood in the stirrups and swept his arm forward. The brassy notes of the trumpet ordered the charge, and the trot

14

increased into the hard pound of hoofs. The wind lashed his face, and again he tasted the exhilaration of living again.

He could hear the guns more plainly, and the lessening distance increased the sound of them. The reports were interposed by the thin, shrill yipping. He swept over the brow of a hill, the forager's line pounding after him. It was all before him; he was coming off of a height, and he had surprise with him. He could congratulate himself now. If he could have ordered every detail to his liking, it would not be better.

Hutson had picked his position well. Fetterman caught an occasional flash of blue uniform in that clump of boulders. Two of them were inordinately still and draped over the boulder before them. Hutson must have caught a glimpse of movement or color that had warned him, for the trees thickened a thousand yards ahead. The boles were dark and shiny, set off against the background of green. If Hutson had ridden into them, he would have been put much harder against it to defend himself. Here he had some protection and an open field of fire in every direction.

Fetterman saw no sign of the horses. Hutson would not have had time to lead them off and picket them. Fetterman surmised that the animals had panicked and bolted at the first outbreak of fire. He would not let that loss concern him right now.

The first moment of commitment seemed to crawl in slow motion. The sheen of light from the naked, red torsos flashed as the Sioux tried to tighten their circle around the nest of boulders. Did they oil themselves before they went into battle? Fetterman pushed the thought aside. It was odd how the trivial occupied a man's mind at a time like this.

An Indian broke out of the moving circle and tried to dart toward the boulders. He hung over one side, and a near miss could have made him change his mind. He turned the horse, and, for a moment, the animal presented a broad side. A cool head directed the defense. Fetterman supposed Hutson had to be given credit for that. No wild bursts of fire wasted ammunition. An aimed shot sought out the pony, and it went down, throwing its rider. The horse skidded several yards before its momentum was spent. It tried to rise, and its front legs threshed against the ground as it struggled to drag its paralyzed hindquarters. Its scream of pain rose higher and higher. Fetterman had seen horses gutshot before, and if a man was near enough to it, he would smell the raw reek of fresh manure, spilled out of its entrails.

The Indian ran in a crouching, twisting run, trying to reach cover, and a giant scythe cut his feet from under him. Fetterman grunted in pure animal pleasure as the figure moved no more.

This was the dream of a battle commander's life. The Sioux were caught between the two blades of a great scissors. Hutson was the lesser one, and Fetterman led the bigger one. The two blades closed with awful efficiency. In that first, vital moment before the blades closed, the Sioux were unaware they were caught.

Fetterman's hasty judgment placed the Sioux at better than fifty warriors trying to close their noose around the boulders. Brashear and Linn had been far wrong in their estimation. Fetterman was still outnumbered, but not enough for him to reconsider his charge.

Bodies, dotting the approaches to the boulders, showed that Hutson had already taken a toll. Hutson couldn't have held them much longer, but he had done his job. He had drawn out the Sioux and checked them until Fetterman brought up the main force.

A wave of blue hit the fringe of the circling Indians and washed over them, destroying their pattern. Savage faces froze in disbelief, then twisted with a new, desperate rage. Sabers slashed and hacked, turning a mounted man into a riderless pony that wheeled and spun in blind panic, adding to the confusion.

An individual never really knew how the entire battle was going. He couldn't see beyond the tiny segment in which he was involved. Fetterman fired his pistol into a distorted face, and the face was snatched from his view. He drove into the Indian pony, driving it out of his path and looked for another target. He fired again and missed, cursing his inaccuracy.

Two forces flung itselves against each other, recoiled, then clashed again. Sabers were the only accurate weapon for this close work. Carbines and war lances were hampered by the confinement, and a war club couldn't get inside the reach of a saber.

Fetterman knew he was losing men. He passed Critchell, and the man's hands gripped an arrow that had been driven clear through him. Critchell's face was agony-twisted, and his face was bloodless. He was losing his struggle to remain in his saddle. He slowly toppled toward the ground as Fetterman went by him.

Fetterman fired until his pistol was empty, then flung it into a howling face. The face rocked back, and when Fetterman flung a glance behind him, another riderless pony was adding to the madness.

No man could say how long those first savage minutes lasted, but it seemed an eternity. A war club was raised to swing down at him, and he tried to duck and whirl out of its path at the same time. The hate-drawn lips were pulled back from teeth, and the face grew larger and larger.

This was the moment that froze a man, and he wanted to yell under his helplessness. A saber cut through the juncture of Indian neck and shoulder. The head lopped to one side, and Murphy yanked his blade free. It was close enough so that Fetterman felt the fine spray of blood moisten his face. He blew out his breath as the war club fell to the ground. Murphy whipped by him, his mouth twisted in a fixed grin, and the saber's blade had changed color.

The wave washed clear through the Sioux, and Fetterman whirled his mount. Those terrible minutes had exacted their toll from both sides. Still forms dotted the ground, and a few knots of dismounted men were locked in hand to hand struggle. An Indian struggled to raise his torso above his shat-

17

tered hips, and a trooper kicked him in the face as he dashed by him.

Fetterman reached the boulders, and Hutson's men were out from behind them. Hutson yelled something that was only a meaningless garble of sound. Fetterman leaned over to snatch a carbine from one of the trooper's hands.

He re-formed the men, closest to him, and drove back into the wavering mass. Pressure broke up the concentrated mass fighting, turning it into individual battle. The Indians were weakening, and the poison of their growing uncertainty showed as they tried to break contact. Indian after Indian wheeled his pony with a single thought in their heads; to get away. Orders couldn't be heard over the yells and thuds of hoofs, but the blue uniforms didn't need them. The taste of triumph filled their mouths, and they didn't need orders.

The cavalry wheeled and came back, still intact as a wave, and the Indians fled in open panic, each only concerned with his safety.

The flush of battle fever raged in Fetterman, but it wasn't enough to overcome instinct and training. The Indians were almost to the thicker trees and digging them out could be too costly.

He jumped to the ground for shooting from the saddle was usually inaccurate. His example reached the dozen troopers nearest him. They threw off with carbines in their hands, and they fired from the kneeling or standing position. He aimed at a fleeing back, and the arms flung out widely before it slid slowly off to one side. Other tongues of fire reached for additional targets, and more riderless ponies galloped on.

The bugler was at Fetterman's side, and he yelled, "Call them back."

Its strident notes reached and turned most of the blue uniforms, chasing after the Sioux. They skidded to a halt and broke off their pursuit. Fetterman's face was black as he watched nine or ten troopers disappear into the trees. Some of them wouldn't come back.

His shirt had changed shade under the sweat of exertion, and he felt its clinging dampness. His chest hurt under the effort of getting fresh air into his lungs.

The battle fever had gone, and only the aftermath remained to lay its heavy, depressive hand on him. He looked at the blue forms, marking the flow and ebb of the fight. It had been costly, and for a moment his eyes refused to make the tabulating. He counted fourteen men down, but five of them were moving. Some of the wounded would probably die and increase the final count, and he had to get those troopers back from their reckless chase into the trees.

His face brightened as he counted twenty-two Indian bodies. The ones, who were stirring, wouldn't be for long, for troopers were moving from one to the next. Murphy dispatched one of them with a saber cut, and the sharp cracks of carbines took care of the others. Fetterman made no attempt to stop it. These were wounded enemies, and he felt no compassion for them.

Hutson joined him, and he still panted as though he had just finished a long run. His face was streaked and smudged, both from the dirt and the soiling of black powder smoke. He bled from a shallow scratch in his cheek, and it emphasized the gauntness of his face. He looked slowly about him, and the hideous count drew the blood from his face.

"My God," he said in a broken voice. "We lost a lot."

Fetterman expected that from a green officer. "Count the Sioux, Mr. Hutson," he snapped. "Then weigh it again." He knew a quick rage at the man. Hutson's words stripped the gloss from his accomplishment.

"We whipped them, Mr. Hutson," he rasped. "Nothing else matters. We gave them a lesson they will remember for a long time. They will think about it before they approach a blue uniform again."

"I lost two more." Hutson's voice was heavy with the cost of it.

Fetterman bit back his savage response. One experience

wouldn't make a battle veteran of this officer. "See to our wounded and report back to me."

He uncapped his canteen before he sat down. He took a long pull from it and let the water trickle down his chin and splash onto his chest. He stuffed his pipe full and lit it, sucking in the smoke. General Cooke would approve of this.

Hutson came back and his voice had a dull timbre. "Mac-Cauley and Masters are dying. The others will recover."

Fetterman let his eyes rest briefly on the troopers administering to the wounded. Even as close to Kearny as they were, it would poise a problem getting the wounded to the stockade.

His cold disapproval of Hutson's reaction would not let him praise him. "Why did you pick your position, Mr. Hutson?"

"We ran across Jennings' body up a way, sir. I saw the Sioux in the edge of the trees. I remembered the boulders and got back to them as fast as I could."

Fetterman wouldn't give him a lift of any kind. "I want to see Jennings, Mr. Hutson."

Hutson shuddered involuntarily. He walked like a much older man.

Fetterman's lips clamped together. Hutson would get over that. Dying was always part of a soldier's wages.

Murphy followed them. Hutson did not have to point out Jennings. The poor, mutilated body lay a hundred yards from the forest's edge. The Sioux has stripped his uniform away, and the uncovered whiteness was an obsenity. The bleeding had stopped, but the red slashes showed how cruelly the knives had worked.

Hutson gagged and turned his head. Fetterman silently raged at him. If Mr. Hutson stayed under his command, he would smash that weakness in him.

Even Murphy was affected by the sight. His breath had a queer whistling, and his jaws were ridged.

"The bloody, butchering savages." Murphy's voice didn't sound the same.

Fetterman eyed him with distaste. "This was the only way they could strip his white supremacy from him."

He heard the hard pound of hoofs and raised his head. Eight men raced out of the trees. That left a man unaccounted for.

They pulled up before him, and he noticed the ghastly shine of their faces, the tight withdrawn line of their mouths. They had looked at terror, and he felt no pity. He thought cynically, they had lost their appetite for their pursuit.

"Where's Addison?" he demanded.

"Two of the Sioux ran him through with lances, Captain," one of them panted. "A bunch of them were gathered up ahead. I guess they stopped when they saw no more were coming after them. There was nothing we could do for Addison."

Fetterman stared at them with flinty eyes. That added another number to his losses. He could find no sympathy for these men. "Next time, you'll listen for the bugle."

He canted his head as he heard the faint notes of a bugle. It came from the direction of Kearny. Carrington must have heard the shots and was sending out a relief column. It erased the urgency of thinking about a counterattack.

"All of you can rest easy," he said coldly. That included Hutson. "A relief column is on the way."

He did not need it, he thought furiously. He amended the thought. He could use its assistance in getting his wounded into Fort Phil Kearny.

CHAPTER THREE

Colonel Henry B. Carrington was sitting behind his desk when Fetterman was called into his office. He was a slender man, with a neatly trimmed beard. He sat very straight as though there was no back to his chair. Fetterman had exchanged but a very few words with him after the two columns had joined on the trail. Fetterman had a preconceived picture of Carrington, and the brief meeting with him had only set his impression of the man's inadequacy. Carrington had been concise and short in his speech, and Fetterman judged it to be a cloak to disguise his unsureness. He saw nothing now that would upgrade his impression.

He knew the colonel's record. Carrington was a lawyer by profession, and Fetterman had heard the man had also taught. Both of the jobs fitted him better, Fetterman thought cynically. Carrington was a reserve officer with little or no basis for the eagles he wore. Cooke must be certain by now that he had picked the wrong man to command a fighting force.

Carrington had raised an Ohio volunteer regiment when the Civil War started. He had known no battle duty. He was an administrative officer, fighting his war from behind a desk. Why did the Army let such men stay in, Fetterman raged inwardly. He hadn't yet seen a reserve officer who was worth his rations. He cursed the inequities of rank, particularly when it was earned by only time. By God, to be commanded by an officer like this ground his soul.

He put a false smile on his face. Carrington hadn't yet

complimented him on his victory, and Fetterman judged jealousy was behind it.

"We taught them a severe lesson, Colonel." Carrington had nothing to do with it. He had been included in that "we" only out of courtesy. "They'll think again before they jump the Army."

The cold façade of Carrington's face didn't crack. "Will they, Captain?" His cheeks were rigid, his eyes blazing.

The false smile disappeared. Fetterman was astounded. The man was struggling to control some passion.

"I don't believe I understand the colonel." It was hard for Fetterman to keep the contempt out of his eyes. He had never seen more flagrant jealousy.

"Counting your wounded, do you realize that you lost better than a third of your command? You were bringing them as reinforcements for Kearny. I need every man I can get."

Fetterman's lips curled. "How would the colonel have handled it?" he asked softly.

The hot rush of blood erased the grayness from Carrington's face. "I would have gotten them here. Some way, I would have—" He broke it off and made a frustrated gesture.

It told Fetterman everything. Here was a man who had been handed a task beyond him, an utterly defeated man.

Fetterman's eyes were frigid. Carrington hadn't yet even welcomed him to Kearny. Let the animosity grow between them; he didn't give a damn.

"Colonel, I have been taught to meet the enemy wherever I could. A handful of savages—" He blew out a ragged breath. "Poorly armed and poorly led. Bow and arrows, lances and war clubs. Not a fifth of them carried rifles."

Carrington studied him. "But your cavalrymen carried Spencer rifles. Outside of the few cavalry I have, my infantry have old single-shot Springfields. How many times have I so notified General Cooke of that?"

The colonel paused momentarily. "Captain, do you really

believe you hurt Red Cloud? That the loss of a few warriors will have anything to do with changing his plans?"

Fetterman wished he could say the acid words that were on his tongue. An officer hurt the enemy every time he could, and he did not mourn over necessary losses. Maybe Carrington thought of his effort as only a drop, but enough of them filled a bucket. He stood at rigid attention, his mouth a thin slash in his face.

Carrington studied him and read something behind the blazing eyes. "Never mind, Captain." A man had never sounded so tired. "Will you step outside and ask the others to come in?"

Fetterman seethed as he walked to the door. Criticism was the last thing he had expected.

He signaled the officers he had brought here and the two civilians to come in. Hutson had had time to clean his face and change to a fresh shirt, and it aroused a hard amusement in Fetterman. That might impress Carrington.

Carrington took salutes from the officers, then extended his hand in welcome. "Gentlemen, I'm sorry this meeting isn't under more propitious aspects. This is Jim Bridger and Portugee Phillips. Please be seated."

The two civilians took chairs, leaving two officers standing. Fetterman's snort almost burst from his lips. It was typical of the laxness with which Carrington commanded.

The civilians had been hired as scouts, Fetterman supposed. He studied them briefly. Neither of them impressed him. Bridger wore a flat-crowned, broad-brimmed hat, which sat squarely on his head. His grizzled beard needed trimming. Fringe decorated his buckskin jacket just below his shoulders, and the garment showed signs of long wear. A smile crinkled Bridger's eyes, and Fetterman had the feeling that the man was aware of his disgust. In Fetterman's experience, a man disciplined himself in his appearance, or he didn't discipline himself in anything.

Bridger looked about for a cuspidor and not finding one,

spit on the floor. The aroma of the sweet brown tobacco he chewed drifted to Fetterman. Carrington let it go unobserved, and that increased Fetterman's rage. It was only a small, additional proof of the way Carrington ran things.

He shifted his gaze to Phillips. This was the man who had impressed Hutson so much.

Portugee Phillips sat in his chair with its back tilted against a wall. His hatbrim was pulled low over his eyes, and Fetterman thought, he doesn't give a damn about what is going on. But he had to give him credit he couldn't give Bridger. Philips took some pride in his appearance. His mustache and short-pointed beard were meticulously trimmed. Fetterman wondered with mild curiosity where Phillips had gotten that odd name. That and his olive-tinted skin was evidence of foreign blood.

Physically, there was little to compare them, less it was in the crow's-feet around the eyes. It seemed that men, who had long looked over wide distances, had that wrinkling. Otherwise, they were not alike, yet there was an odd similarity in the two. All excess flesh had been pared away, and they were steel-thewed. Fetterman could appreciate physical fitness. He wished the kind of men the Army was getting was like them.

"Gentlemen." Carrington called for their attention. "Bridger is one of our scouts. He has led many an expedition for the Army out of Laramie. I couldn't prevail upon Portugee to take a like position." His smile at Phillips had a wry quality. "He prefers to be one of our drivers."

"And a damned good one," Bridger said. "He can handle anything on hoofs. Portugee, I guess you've seen enough of the Sioux."

Phillips' soft grunt signified nothing.

"Captain," Carrington said, "I want you to tell them every detail."

Fetterman accepted the role with relish. At least he could expect approval from the civilians. From Bridger's words they had an equal dislike of the savages.

He embellished every detail, stressing how he had whipped numerical superiority. He finished by saying, "They ran like whipped dogs. I wish we could have killed every one of them. If you could see what they did to Jennings—" A shake of his head completed the sentence.

He changed his mind and described it vividly with a sadistic satisfaction. That would turn Carrington's stomach. "Those butchers weren't satisfied with slashing his body. They hacked off his hands and feet."

Phillips thumbed back his hatbrim. "Captain, every man who's been out here very long has seen that," he drawled. "Lopping off hands and feet is part of their religion."

Fetterman's face was incredulous. What damned nonsense was this?

"It's a mark of their respect for a fighting man." The front legs of Phillips' chair hit the floor with a small bang. "They wanted to be sure your man was handicapped in case they meet him in the Hereafter. He was scalped too, wasn't he?"

Anger twisted Fetterman's face. "He was," he said coldly. Let Phillips explain that away. He had never listened to such drivel.

Phillips nodded. "That will help Jennings cross the Shadow Waters without any trouble."

"Why, goddamn it," Fetterman exploded. He stopped at a warning look from Carrington.

"You pride yourself on doing a hell of a job, don't you, Captain?" Phillips' voice showed no stress, but there seemed to be a new tension in him. "Let me tell you exactly what you did. Red Cloud has two, maybe three thousand warriors. He's sworn to wipe out every new fort the white man built. He's set fire to the plains. You just added some more fuel."

Fetterman felt as though he was choking. He didn't give a damn whether or not Carrington liked it, but he had to say what he felt.

"Are all of you afraid of him?" His rage was evident on his

face. "By God, I'm not. Give me eighty good men, and I'll cut a swath through his whole damned nation."

Bridger and Phillips looked at each other. Fetterman didn't miss the exchange of shaking heads. It wasn't hard to see why General Cooke had grown so impatient with Carrington, if he followed their advice. He had every right to it.

"If the colonel will excuse me," he said icily.

Carrington gave him a weary nod. "Dismissed."

Fetterman stalked out, and the other officers followed him.

A long silence followed, and Carrington showed his distress. "He'll learn," he said weakly.

"Maybe," Bridger said noncommittedly.

"If he's got enough time," Phillips added. "Is that all, Colonel?"

Carrington nodded, and both men rose. Phillips' eyes slid away from his face. He didn't envy Carrington the load he was carrying.

Bridger spat another amber stream when he got outdoors. His grin held no amusement. "What do you think of him, Portugee?"

Phillips' eyes had a faraway look, and he shrugged. "I think he'll get a lot of men killed."

CHAPTER FOUR

Phillips was scowling as he stepped into his cabin. It was built against the outer wall of the fort, and the fort's proximity should give him a feeling of security. But after listening to Captain Fetterman, that feeling was gone.

He was barely medium height, and most men, in the territory, topped him. He was called "little" or "Portugee," and only a foolish man dared use either in a derogatory manner. He was stocky and well-muscled, and he had the quick, easy movement of a cat. He was equally capable with pistol, rifle, or knife. He wasn't given to idle talk, and when he spoke, it was usually only in answer to a direct question. His Portuguese blood showed in the olive tint of his skin. He had been born John Phillips on the Portuguese island of Faial, one of the Azores, and he was in his middle thirties. He was nearly grown when he landed on the western coast of America, and had quickly picked up the unique skills to survive in this new country.

His cheekbones were high, the nose as thin as the blade of a hatchet. His eyes were dark, almost black, and he kept his mustache and beard meticulously trimmed. If he had a vanity, it showed there. He was a quiet and dependable man, showing ability as miner and prospector, hunter and trapper, woodcutter and teamster. He had gone through the California gold rush and had hunted and prospected in Nevada, Idaho, and Montana. He was married and had two children, a boy and a girl. His family had gone everyplace with him, and asking him about the recklessness of taking them into dangerous country would have brought a puzzled frown to his face. Protecting them was as natural to him as breathing, and he had no doubt about his ability to take care of them. His family was one of the first to go up the Bozeman Trail in 1864, and he was back in 1865 and again in the summer of 1866. Jim Wheatley and Isaac Fisher had joined him on the last trip, both men seasoned in staying alive. They had found traces of gold along the side creeks of the Powder River country, and it was in enough quantity to say that it could be turned into a profitable thing. But it had been trespassing in the forbidden country of the Teton Sioux.

The last treaty meeting at Laramie had been a farce, and Red Cloud had upset a man's plans. Portugee had watched the gathering of the various Sioux tribes, the Tetons, the Brûlés, the Santees, the Oglala, the Miniconjou, and the Hunkpapas. To make it worse the Cheyennes had joined them. No white man knew exactly how many of them had answered Red Cloud's call, but it was a formidable number. It had been time to get out of that country, and Portugee had made tracks out of there.

In a way Portugee didn't blame Red Cloud. The finding of gold had brought in its usual rush of whites, and it was a real threat to Red Cloud's last hunting ground. The Sioux chieftain had made a real effort to stop short of war. At first, he had only turned back the emigrants going up the trail, but that hadn't been enough. Gold was the lure, and the whites had pressed on in greater and greater numbers. The raids and killing had started shortly afterward. Portugee could see both sides. The killings had brought outraged cries from Congress, and he guessed the Army had the problem of protecting the emigrants tossed into their laps. He felt sorry for Colonel Carrington. The man was trying to do the job handed him. Was he big enough was the question.

Hattie Phillips was stirring a bubbling stew over a stove, and its good aroma drifted to Phillips. She was a small woman of sturdy stock. Portugee could not remember a complaint from her. She flashed him a smile over her shoulder, then it quickly faded. At times, it startled him to realize she could read his thoughts when he was positive nothing showed on his face, or no gesture gave him away.

His feeling for her was deeply embedded, though he was rarely able to put it into words. She wasn't an outstanding beauty by any classic standard, but her kind grew slowly and steadily on a man. How blind he had been when he first thought her plain. A man learned to treasure her kind, for she was always there for whatever need made its demand. Her eyes were deep and knowing, and he had seen them change shades to meet her mood. Her cheeks were no longer soft and round, and the memory of them brought its little pang. He was responsible for those cheeks thinning, for the skin weathering and toughening. He thought with regret that he had dragged her over a lot of rough country, but she would have it no other way.

"No trouble," he assured her, but it didn't quite convince her. "Where are the kids?" The boy was eight years old and beginning to look like him. The girl, of six, was named after her. In disposition, they were taking after her, and he was glad of that. She was instilling her balance and serenity in them. He hoped they would never have the quick, hot flash of his temper.

"They're playing in the fort, Portugee."

He had given strict orders they were never to go farther outside of the fort than the cabins, and it was always a relief to learn they were obeying him. He had received Carrington's permission to build two small cabins, just off of the main gate, against the outer stockade. Sentries were always on the walkways above the cabins, and at least, it gave the illusion of security. Many a night he had gone to sleep wondering if it was enough. Wheatley and his wife occupied the other cabin, and Fisher lived in first one cabin, then the other.

Fisher sat at the table, and his eyes had an appraising look. "You got a mouth full of something bad?"

He had the same perceptiveness as Hattie but perhaps in

31

a lesser degree. It was an insight given to people who lived closely together.

Portugee made a wry face. "Does it show that much? I just met some of the new officers."

Hattie turned and was watching him. The tightness in her face wasn't new; she only allowed it to show now.

Fisher grinned. "Didn't they impress you?"

"That Captain Fetterman is a firebrand," Portugee said soberly. "Give him eighty men and he can ride clear through the Sioux nation."

The grin faded from Fisher's face. "That's the kind we need all right." He was taller than Portugee. Their faces were dissimilar in features and molding, but the same look was there. He had the same restless seeking of eye and spirit. He and Portugee and Wheatley fitted well together.

"What do you think, Portugee?"

"I think I made a mistake in wintering here instead of going on to Laramie." Portugee felt an unusual heaviness of mood. It happened to him every time he met an officer who knew it all without the necessity of learning. Maybe the high wages of seventy-five dollars a month, offered by Carrington, had tempted him. Fisher and Wheatley had hired on as scouts. Portugee had been interested only in a driving job.

"Portugee, do you think it's wise to pull up now?"

"Two hundred and thirty-six miles is a hell of a distance under these conditions, Isaac. Red Cloud has drawn a tighter ring around Kearny. He swears he'll see it burned down. I think Carrington realizes what he's up against. He had to staff Fort Reno with half of his original command. He's been yelling his head off for newer and more weapons and men." He allowed himself a brief smile. "I think our Henrys are the main reason for offering us a job. What the colonel got today wasn't nearly enough to carry out Cooke's orders. Carrington hasn't got enough weapons or men to attack Red Cloud."

Fisher's eyes were pensive. "Meeting the Sioux on their own ground, destroying their villages, and whipping their fighting men is one hell of an order."

32

Portugee nodded gloomy agreement.

Hattie set a tin cup of steaming coffee before him, and his callused hand didn't flinch from the metal's heat. He thanked her with his eyes. He had given her a new burden of worry, and he swore at himself.

"It'll turn out all right, Hattie. Red Cloud will nip at us, but he won't try to take the fort. He knows it would cost him too much. Carrington's got enough men to hold it." He made one provision: if he doesn't try to obey some of those ridiculous orders he gets.

He changed the subject. "You eating with us tonight, Isaac?"

Fisher's grin came back. "I checked what the Wheatleys are having for supper. Yours smells better."

"Good. I'll get the kids. How soon will supper be ready, Hattie?"

"Not more than a half-hour."

He nodded and walked outside. He thought he would probably find the kids around the stables. Horses fascinated them, particularly Carrington's thoroughbred, Gray Eagle. Red Cloud had seen the animal and coveted it at Laramie. Portugee didn't blame the Indian. He wouldn't mind having that thoroughbred himself.

He walked through the main gate. Carrington had built well in Fort Phil Kearny. The stockade wall was made of peeled logs, placed vertically with one end set deep in the ground. Portugee judged the pointed ends were fourteen feet high. It was set on the junction of Little Piney and Big Piney creeks. Their waters flowed to join Clear Creek, a tributary of the Powder. The fort had ample water. Portugee knew the road to both creeks, for he had made a million trips hauling water from them. If it wasn't that, he was hauling logs and wood. A driver earned his seventy-five dollars a month.

Blockhouses were at every corner, built above the palisades, and they would be strong points of defense. A howitzer was on each platform in the corners, and their range commanded the cleared approaches in all directions. It was said that Carrington was the only one who really knew how to handle that ordnance. The lack of training in others was a bad mistake. The Indians feared the howitzers. They called them "the guns that speak with a loud voice."

He nodded to the sentries on the gate, noting the old, single-shot Springfield rifles they carried. Carrington was worried about adequate ammunition for them. He had other worries on top of that. He knew he wasn't getting in enough target practice. Most of the troopers couldn't hit the stockade walls, if they were surrounded by them. The training had been slighted by the urgency of the building.

It took a hell of a lot of building to erect a fort. Portugee passed the administration building, the magazine, the commissary. Quartermaster supplies had its separate building. The harness room, the stables, and the farrier's area were in a far corner. The barracks, the mess halls, and the kitchen took up one wall, while the officers' quarters and those of the commanding officer were on an adjoining wall. His eyes ran over the saw mill, a granary, and bakery, and he hadn't begun to name all of the buildings. Nobody could doubt that the Army had come to stay. Only Red Cloud and a couple of thousand Indians, Portugee thought.

He heard the strains of a military band at the far end of the parade ground. It was time for retreat. Carrington liked his martial music. Portugee grunted. He could see nothing more useless than a band on an Indian campaign; unless those musicians were damned good at doubling with a rifle. He had another harsh criticism for retreat and reveille. The Army could waste a lot of time on their military formations.

He nodded to several women he passed. While he was about it, he might as well add another criticism to his list. He didn't approve of Carrington allowing wives to accompany their husbands into hostile territory. That drew a self-rebuke. You brought your woman along too, didn't you?

He stopped for a moment to exchange a few words with Mrs. Grummond. She was a slender woman, with the joy of life bubbling up within her. She had a gay, infectious laugh that made a man grin in appreciation. Another woman like Hattie, he thought, following her husband out here. She had lived in the East, and she had come to Kearny with her husband, Lieutenant George Grummond.

"Do you think it's going to snow again, Mr. Phillips?"

He squinted at the pale, watery sun. Clouds were beginning to scud up over the hills. "I wouldn't be surprised."

"Oh, I hope so. I love the snow."

Not Wyoming snows, he thought drily. She's speaking of Eastern snows. He would not try to dampen her happiness with the truth. She was an attractive woman, and her blue eyes went with her blond hair. Something Hattie had told him pounded at him. Despite the slenderness of youth, Mrs. Grummond was pregnant. He couldn't see it, but a woman's intuition would know. "It's in her eyes," Hattie had said. Maybe so, he thought. They're shining, all right.

"Have you seen the kids, Mrs. Grummond?"

"I passed them a moment ago, Mr. Phillips. They were at the stables."

He thanked her and moved on. He hoped nothing that could mar her happiness would ever happen to her.

The kids were still at the stables. They were at Gray Eagle's stall, watching him with fascinated eyes. He was one hell of an animal. Portugee suspected he had the same brightness in his eyes whenever he looked at the horse. He had never had the chance to be around a thoroughbred much before. It was too bad that the cavalry wasn't all mounted on such animals. Gray Eagle could run an Indian pony off its hoofs any time.

"You kids get on home for supper," he said. He was sure of their reluctance to go, but they rarely gave him an argument. He swatted the boy's bottom with an affectionate hand and watched them break into a run. The girl was outdistanced in a half-dozen strides.

He started to follow them, and Captain James Powell

hailed him. "Hold up, Portugee." Portugee turned and waited.

He had liked the man from his first meeting with him. Powell was a long-legged man, straight in the back and narrow in the flanks. His eyes studied a man, but Portugee had never seen disdain in them. The first impression was that he was a cautious man, but that was wrong. It was only patient reserve in those gray eyes. Powell had been out in this country long enough to know something about it, and he was an easy learner.

"Did you meet the new officers?" he asked.

Portugee thought the subtle shading in Powell's tone really asked had he met Fetterman.

Portugee grinned. "I met him. He's an impatient man. He's wondering what's holding you people up."

Powell said a few choice oaths.

Again, Portugee was struck by the similarity between Powell and Carrington. They were carrying the same load.

"Portugee, didn't today convince Fetterman that the Sioux will fight?" He wasn't doing much in disguising his dislike for the man.

"Not very well, Captain."

Powell spat on the ground as though he had to get rid of a bad taste. "He believes like Omaha does. The Sioux won't fight."

"But that's not your belief?"

"It isn't." Powell's voice had an edge. "I was at the last treaty at Laramie. The chiefs, who did sign, are old and tired. The Laramie Loafers, we called them. Hanging around for another handout from the government. The young, hotheaded chiefs stalked out without touching pen to paper. Chief One Horn and Spotted Tail left as mad as poisoned dogs. The young war chief, Crazy Horse, is joining Red Cloud."

Portugee's eyes were reflective. "It was a sorry treaty."

"It was. The commissioners had to have something to report to Washington. They couldn't have a failure on their record. The treaty says there will be no war."

"It looks like both of us picked the wrong post, Captain."

Powell's smile was strained. "I didn't have much choice, Portugee. Neither do the poorly trained recruits we're getting. Will I see you at the sutler's tonight?"

Portugee nodded. He usually dropped in for a drink or two. It kept a man from living too much with his thoughts.

"Good." Powell whirled and strode away.

There went a good man. Portugee weighed what Powell said and made his evaluation. A man could serve under him and have some hope of coming back.

CHAPTER FIVE

A glint of mischief was in Hattie Phillips' eyes as she asked, "Shall I be ready to help you into bed?"

Portugee hoped he impressed her with his display of outrage. "You can't point out a time when you had to help me. Woman, I pride myself on my ability to carry liquor." He appealed to Fisher for support. "Isaac, did you ever see me under?"

Fisher glanced at Hattie, then at Portugee. He was a born diplomat. "Let's say you might have been close to it a couple of times."

Hattie's ringing laugh followed them to the door.

They stopped by Wheatley's cabin, and he joined them. He was the tallest of the three and as fair as Portugee was dark.

"What did you think of the new officers, Portugee?"

Portugee frowned. He meant Fetterman. Everybody who asked him that question seemed to have the same meaning.

"I came out tonight to forget him."

Wheatley laughed and whacked him on the shoulder.

The sutler's store was the meeting club of the post. Laughter and banter filled the air. Portugee glanced about the room. If there was an empty table, he didn't see it.

Amos Lyford, the sutler, greeted them with profuse words. He had a bad habit of talking too much. Portugee paid no attention to it, and he doubted that Fisher or Wheatley did either. They had been in a sutler's store a lot of times, too.

Lyford's eyes were on the small size, and the fat creases

of flesh were encroaching on them. He could never quite hold them steady when another man looked at him. His face had a greasy shine as though too much fat was packed under his hide. He charged exorbitant prices for everything, and he served bad liquor. Portugee didn't begrudge him too much for either, though he wouldn't trust the man as far as he could see him. Lyford freighted his goods out here, and he took all of the risks. Indians would be in seventh heaven, if they could get their hands on Lyford's shabby goods. One successful raid, and he could be wiped out.

Soldiers didn't complain either of the prices charged, mainly because they could go no other place. This broke the routine that made up their days. A soldier's life was a monotonous and grim one, and the hours spent here let him forget it for a little while. The sad part of it was that a soldier's pay was small, a sutler's prices high, and a soldier's money always ran short before the month ended.

"Captain Powell is waiting for you," Lyford said.

Portugee saw him, then, sitting by himself at a table at the far end of the room. They walked over, and Powell asked before they sat down, "What will you have?"

Portugee grimaced as he pulled out a chair. "Have we got a choice?"

They didn't. Lyford served one brand of whiskey, raw and powerful. It had authority once it got past a man's palate.

Powell grinned and raised a hand to Kathy Lyford.

She caught it and threaded her way through the tables. Hands reached out to detain her, and she laughingly avoided them. She couldn't be more than nineteen years old, and she had the bloom of youth. She wasn't an outstanding beauty, but she had several fine features. She had a mass of shining blond hair that fell below her shoulders, and her eyes were as blue as a clear May sky. She had a full and pouting mouth, and she moved with a flaunt of her hips that could not fail to attract male attention. Added to that was the fact that she was the only single woman on the post, and it was an irresistible lure. Her type was always a worry to married women, and she drew some hard words from some of them.

Portugee watched her approach with amusement. He wouldn't blame lonely men. Her youth couldn't fail to make its clarion call. She had an instinctive knowledge of handling men, and as far as he had observed, she hadn't signaled out any particular one to give her attention. She was Amos Lyford's daughter, and her mother had died several years before. A man could censure Lyford for bringing her out here, but Portugee supposed Lyford had no other way of making a living. It was amazing that none of Lyford's grossness showed in her. She was lucky that most of her inheritance had come from her mother.

Her eyes roamed over them in that intimate way some women acquired, or were born with. Portugee didn't get that treatment. Early, she had realized she was wasting it.

"Whiskey, Kathy," Powell ordered. "She's going to drive whatever man she marries crazy," he said as she walked away.

Portugee shrugged. It wasn't his problem. Powell could be wrong, if the man she picked was strong-willed and heavy-handed.

He let his eyes roam over the room. The air was foggy with smoke, and the babble of talk assailed a man's ears. His eyes stopped at a table, a dozen feet from them. It was packed with officers, and Fetterman seemed to dominate the talk. He knew the two captains, Tenedor Ten Eyck and Frederick Brown. He had met some of the junior officers in Carrington's office, but their names hadn't stuck in his head. Lieutenant Grummond was there, and Portugee's eyes picked up a speculative shine. Grummond appeared as engrossed in Fetterman's talk as the others. It caused a mild disappointment in Portugee.

Kathy came back with the whiskey, and Powell asked, "Has it improved any, Kathy?"

"Three or four drinks, and it won't matter," she said tartly.

41

Powell sipped at his glass, and he looked at Fetterman's table. That was a tinge of sourness in his face.

"You've talked with him," Portugee said softly.

The sourness increased in Powell. "Yes, he doesn't need any of the rest of us."

"I told Portugee he sounds like quite a man." His grin belied his words.

"He'll get other chances to prove it," Powell snapped.

That was sure, Portugee thought. Every detail that left the fort would be under Red Cloud's fire. The horses had to be grazed to preserve the hay stacks, wood and daily water had to be brought in. Red Cloud would pare at this one and that one. It could be a simple matter, if Carrington could hold all of his force and never have to venture out. But it couldn't be left that way. It was small wonder that every casualty was another stone on his back.

"Who's taking the horses out in the morning?" he asked.

"I am. Mr. Hutson volunteered, too."

Was that surprise in Powell's voice? It could be. Hutson showed a lot of eagerness. He had just gone through a tough fight this afternoon.

"You've talked with him?"

Powell nodded.

"How did he impress you?"

"The only thing wrong with him now is inexperience. He's willing to learn."

Powell had made his judgment. He didn't name names, but it was an assessment for one man and against another. That was just about the way Portugee would rate it.

"Here he is now," Powell said. He stood and called, "Over here, Tom."

Portugee looked to see if Fetterman might contest that. After all, he and Hutson had arrived together, and they had known the violent moments that binds men together, or forever puts a cleavage between them. Fetterman made no effort to hail Hutson. Was that a glitter in his eyes? At this distance, Portugee couldn't be sure. One thing was apparent;

42

Fetterman had no intention of calling Hutson over to his table.

Hutson walked to them, and that could have been an uncertainty in his manner.

"Tom, do you know these three?" Powell asked.

"I met them at Laramie." Hutson's handshake was firm enough without trying to impress anybody.

He sat down, and Portugee was curious to know Fetterman's reaction to the meeting in Carrington's office. From Powell's tone, he knew there was no love lost between the men. Fetterman wouldn't appreciate Hutson sitting down at this table.

Hutson looked around at the glasses. "I'll have the same."

"You won't like it," Portugee said. He grinned as Hutson's eyebrows rose. "I'm not saying you can't have it." In his opinion Hutson had earned whatever he wanted by today's work. "I'm just stating a fact."

Hutson had an attractive, boyish grin. "That bad, huh? I'll still try it. I'm the hardheaded type."

Portugee beckoned Kathy to their table.

Her eyes picked out Hutson when she was twenty feet away, and all the way over here, they didn't leave his face.

"Kathy, this is Mr. Hutson. He just got here today. He's another new member of our club."

Kathy didn't respond to his mild humor. In fact, he doubted she heard anything beyond Hutson's name.

Portugee didn't miss the meeting of their eyes. Eyes talked to eyes in a secret language of their own, and no outsider would understand it. But it did produce a crackling of lightning without the noise. He saw color stealing into her face.

"Hello, Kathy." Hutson's voice was husky. "I'll have whiskey."

He waited until she walked away. "She married?" He tried to make it casual. "I didn't see a ring."

"She isn't," Portugee said.

He saw the darkening in Hutson's eyes. Her status usually had a special connotation on an Army post.

43

Portugee grinned at Powell. "He's got an evil mind, Captain. She works for her father. She's got a right to be here."

The darkening disappeared from Hutson's eyes, and the color flowed up from his collar. "I thought—I—" He stumbled over his words.

Powell's eyes crinkled at the corners, but his voice was severe. "Lieutenant, didn't they teach you at the Point never to make your evaluation on just appearances?"

Portugee, Fisher, and Wheatley roared at Hutson's expression, and Powell was delighted.

Hutson tried to find a defense, failed, then said, "Oh, go to hell."

Kathy came back with the whiskey, and this was a different girl. She looked flustered, and a man could almost guess her thoughts. Had they been talking about her? She set down the whiskey, picked up the payment for it, and hurried away.

Portugee watched her with speculative eyes. This Hutson had something that she had seen, and it had made its impact. Maybe he had better treat him with more respect.

Hutson stared after her with a stricken face. "I've got to apologize to her."

He half-rose, and Portugee caught his arm. "Are you going to tell her what you were thinking?"

Hutson sank back into his chair. "I guess not," he muttered. He downed his whiskey in a single gulp.

This was reckless drinking, even for a man familiar with Lyford's whiskey. Portugee waited for the reaction with interest. Taking that glassful in a single drink turned into a raw, brutal club, pounding Hutson's palate. He grabbed for his throat, and for a moment, it looked as though he couldn't get his breath. His eyes watered, and he choked and gasped.

Portugee's eyes were bright with amusement. Hutson wouldn't die, though he might feel like it at the moment. Hutson had just learned from another experience; not to treat sutler whiskey carelessly. He'll do, he thought.

He stayed for another round, and Hutson made an elaborate process of ordering another drink, trying to detain Kathy, but she wouldn't stay. Portugee had never seen her so disturbed. She had lost her usual control, and it had half-frightened, half-angered her. He would like to stay around and watch developments between Hutson and the woman, but that could take up too much of the night.

He pushed back his empty glass and stood. "I promised Hattie I wouldn't stay long. Anybody coming with me?" He knew Hutson's answer before he opened his mouth.

"I just got here," Hutson protested.

The others went with Portugee. He looked back from the door. Hutson sat alone, his eyes following Kathy wherever she went.

"I hope he gets in before reveille," Powell said in a grumpy voice.

Portugee grinned. Hutson would probably lose some sleep, but at his age he could afford the loss. Somebody else was interested in what Hutson was doing. Fetterman split his attention between Hutson and Kathy.

It was none of his damned business what's going on between them, Portugee thought with some heat. He had a strong hunch that in some way Fetterman would make it his business. Fetterman was a vain man, if his first impression wasn't wrong. A vain man could not stand to be topped in anything.

He looked at Powell, and Powell slowly nodded. He saw everything that was going on. Hutson has a friend, a friend that might be able to do him some good. Powell's rank could be a bulwark for Hutson. But how strong that bulwark was depended upon the date of rank of Powell and Fetterman. Rank was jealously protected. Portugee had seen just a few days of seniority make the difference.

He said his "good night" to Powell and walked home with Fisher and Wheatley.

His silence prompted Wheatley into words. "You must have something heavy on your mind."

45

Portugee gave him a twisted grin. "You'd think Red Cloud would be enough to occupy a man's mind, wouldn't you?"

Fisher had missed some of the subtle shadings that had gone on back there. "He's sure as hell big enough to fill my head."

CHAPTER SIX

The bugle at reveille awakened Portugee. The light wasn't yet strong. Hattie stirred restlessly but did not awaken.

He debated upon trying to go back to sleep, then decided against it. He got up and dressed noiselessly and picked up his Spencer. Without it he would feel as undressed as without his pants.

The boy was sitting up, and Portugee frowned a warning at him. A soft smile was on his lips as the boy settled back.

Sleepy ranks were forming out on the parade ground as Portugee walked into the fort, and sergeants called the rolls. He heard many a foreign-sounding name, and some of them were jawbreakers. Those men were not only new to Indian fighting but Portugee suspected many of them hadn't been long in the United States.

The sergeants completed the roll call and received permission from attending officers to dismiss the men. Portugee had always wondered why the Army got up so early when it spent so much of its day in idleness. It was rush to meet reveille, rush to breakfast, then sit around for hours doing nothing.

The ranks broke as men hurried for the mess hall. Portugee had no particular desire for breakfast for last night's supper was still with him, but he would welcome hot coffee.

He joined the lines of men, waiting for the mess hall to open. Some of them joked and laughed, the others had long faces and were silent. He guessed the Lord had made men in two classes: the happy ones and the sour ones.

47

The door was opened, and the file of men shuffled forward. The officers had the tables at the front of the hall. Powell and Hutson sat a table across the aisle from Fetterman and other officers. Fetterman's face had a heavy, somber cast, and it could be the results of last night's drinking, or the worsening of relationship between him and Powell and Hutson. Portugee would say the latter.

Hutson must have stayed up late, and it showed in his heavy-lidded eyes. Portugee did not let his smile show. A man had to learn he had to pay a price for just about everything.

He sat down across from them and grimaced at the food on their trays. It didn't even look appetizing. His stomach didn't adjust to most of the breakfasts the Army served.

He sipped at his coffee, realizing this was a mistake, too. He should have waited for Hattie's coffee.

"Are you almost through, Mr. Hutson?" Powell asked.

Most of the food on Hutson's tray was untouched. His mind was obviously elsewhere.

"I'm ready, Captain."

"How's the grass along Little Piney?" Portugee asked.

Powell frowned. "It's going. But we need every mouthful they can graze to save hay."

"Good luck, Captain."

Powell quirked his eyebrows. "Sure."

Portugee finished his coffee in a gulp and was only a couple of steps behind them as they left. He wanted to see those horses taken out. They shouldn't be out of sight of the fort all the time they were grazing.

He climbed a ladder to a walkway and nodded to the sentry, who passed him. Even the threat of danger couldn't keep a man from becoming bored at the dragging time on sentry duty. It was affecting this man for he looked half asleep.

He watched the horses pour out through the opened gates. Their heads went down as soon as they reached the grass. Some of the herders lolled in their saddles, and Portugee swore at them. He knew what they were thinking. They were within view of the fort. But yesterday's events should be vivid enough in their minds to erase all carelessness. Powell and Hutson were constantly on the move, jacking up first one man, then another, but it was hard to overcome the boredom of another job nobody wanted.

The horse herd was almost out of the clearing, and the creek was just beyond them. The rising sun was just above the rim of the earth, and its strengthening rays were blinding. Portugee wasn't sure whether or not he actually saw movement in the east, or sensed it. Whatever it was, the pickets didn't pick it up. Then he heard the shrill, sharp yipping.

The Sioux poured out of the sun and were in among the horses before the troopers were fully aware they were on them. These were magnificent horsemen, and they could ride around clumsy troopers before they could think of wheeling.

Color clashed and recoiled, like a kaleidoscope madly turned. Motion ran together, heaved up, and fell back, and now it had lost all sense of direction. No man could number the Sioux that made their run out of the early, angry eye of the dawn sun.

This was the moment when panic could jerk the bowels out of a man. It was a typical Sioux raid, devastating because of its unexpectedness, and a man fought his stunned mind to force it into admitting that it was happening. But dear God, this was still in the cleared approaches to the fort in view of it.

Portugee groaned and swore as he watched the first sweep of the Sioux smash the feeble resistance before them. He doubted there were more than twenty of them, and after the first violent clash, a pattern became definite. The Sioux were after horses, rather than scalps.

He heard rifle fire, but it was disorganized. He put no blame on Powell or Hutson. They had their hands full from keeping the panic from sweeping into a rout.

He saw two horsemen smash together, and a blue uniform toppled to the ground. The Indian drove on without a look behind him. It was additional proof of what they wanted.

The Sioux kept to a precast plan, and they waved blankets and screamed as they rode into the horses.

No horses could stand up to this, and the apparitions shattered their nerves. They broke and scattered into a dozen segments. A large bunch dashed toward the creek and splashed through it, their hoofs throwing back a fan of water. Others broke to the north and east, and the Sioux fell in behind them, their object accomplished.

Powell kept his head, letting those bunches go. If he had tried to recover those horses, he would have made a serious mistake. Portugee imagined Powell was yelling out his lungs, but Powell reacted well. He collected a dozen men and cut off the horses that would have followed the others. The thin line turned them and headed them at a dead run toward the fort. Powell saved something out of the promised disaster.

This was the first chance Portugee had for a clear shot, and his rage demanded some repayment. He was vaguely aware that rifles barked all along the sentry walk, but those old Springfields would never reach that far. He sighted on a Sioux back. This Indian had straightened up, and that was his mistake. It was a long shot, and if Portugee had to call it, he would say it was a wasted bullet. He squeezed the trigger, and that Indian went even straighter, sticking tight for a half-dozen more strides. Then he disappeared as though a giant hand wiped him off of the pony. Portugee searched for another target and decided against spending another bullet on a doubtful target.

The gates swung wide, and horses and men streamed through. Horses fanned out once inside, each animal running its own crazy path.

Horror squeezed Portugee's guts. One of those horses ran directly at his little girl, and she was frozen in terror. Every one of those horses ran in blind fear, and Portugee doubted this one could even see his girl.

He yelled to release the horrible pressure, and as he jumped to the ground he knew he could not possibly reach the spot in time. A futile thought ran through his mind. How many times had he warned the kids not to get close to the horses?

A slim woman ran at a tangent across the course of those maddened hoofs. She swooped up the girl without breaking stride. For a moment it looked as though she would get clear, then an animal's shoulder brushed her, sending her spinning. She tried to regain her balance, and she couldn't make it. She fell with the girl in her arms.

Portugee pounded toward her. Mrs. Grummond was struggling to get to her feet, and he reached both hands to pull her up.

"Are you all right?" The concern in his voice made it ragged. The information Hattie had given him pounded at his mind.

Her face was smudged, and her dress was torn. She gulped in great breaths, and he could feel her shake in her arms.

"I just fell," she assured him. "I'm fine."

Portugee's daughter was crying hard with the release of her terror. Mrs. Grummond hugged her tighter and said, "Honey, it's all right. It's all over." Her bright, blond hair was in disarray, and it covered the girl's head.

Portugee was washed by two emotions, his tremendous relief and his anger. How many times had he told those kids to stay away from the horses.

He took her from Mrs. Grummond's arms and hugged her with one arm while his other hand felt over arms and legs. He didn't find anything broken. "You're all right," he said over and over.

He looked at Mrs. Grummond. "You saved her life," he said huskily.

She shrugged an expressive shoulder. "I was the closest," she said simply.

It was a brave but reckless thing to do, but how could he censure.

Color flooded her face as the knowledge that he knew her condition hit her. "Everything's all right."

51

He held the girl in one arm and took Mrs. Grummond's wrist. Lieutenant Grummond had to know about this.

"Let me take you home."

The shakiness was still in her for it showed in her ragged laughter. "He'll have a fit."

Portugee imagined that he would. It was enough to put concern in a husband. The runaway horses were bunched in a corner of the stockade, and a line of mounted troopers pressed them harder. It would take more work to settle them down and get them back to the stable. Carrington would know a new wave of despair when the tabulation of this raid reached him. One event after another relentlessly ground him.

Portugee's eyes were grave. "I'll never be able to pay this back."

She tried to say it lightly. "Forget it, Mr. Phillips."

She meant it, but it didn't lessen his debt.

He saw Lieutenant Grummond running toward them. Grummond would be wild until she could settle him down. Portugee imagined that the least he would do would be to have her examined by the post surgeon. He would send Hattie over to see Mrs. Grummond as soon as he got his daughter home. If there was anything that should be done, Hattie would know. He could not let go of his last worry until Hattie reported to him.

CHAPTER SEVEN

Portugee hitched a team of mules to a wagon. Somebody had to go out there and get Tillery's body. He climbed up onto the seat and lifted the reins. Sure, he would be happier if a detail accompanied him, but the fort was pretty upset now. Sergeants still swore at horses that were still stubborn, and all of the animals weren't yet stabled. Quite a few of them were darker shades of color. It didn't take much exertion to bring out the sweat on a horse, particularly if it had been used hard and was upset. Portagee didn't think any Sioux were lurking around, but no man could guess at what they would do next. He would make this chore just as fast as he could.

Powell saw him and rode over. "Where do you think you're going?" His eyes were smoky, and some inner agitation still worked on him.

"I thought I'd go out and get Tillery," Portugee said mildly.

"I hadn't forgotten about him," Powell snapped.

Portugee didn't imagine he had.

"Wait until I get these damned horses settled down, and I'll take a detail out with you."

Portugee shrugged. "Suit yourself."

Powell dreaded something, and Portugee wondered if it was the report he had to make to Carrington. He knew he would dread it if he was in Powell's boots.

He waited fifteen minutes until Powell and his detachment fell in around him. Hutson was part of it, and a strain made his face gaunt and harsh. He's had a rough arrival, Portugee thought, as he put the mules into motion.

He looked back after he had driven through the gates, and the walkway along that side of the stockade was jammed. Every step of the way would be under the eye of the fort. But then, so had the grazing horses. Fetterman was just above him, and that could be a sardonic pleasure on his dark face. If Powell saw it, it wouldn't help this rage. Portugee was certain Powell was flogging himself, but who could have done better? Fetterman probably had a different answer to that question.

Tillery's face showed that he had died hard. But then, a man usually did under these conditions. At least, he hadn't been stripped and mutilated.

Two men swung down and lifted Tillery into the wagon. Tillery would be buried inside the fort. Its graveyard was growing larger.

The Indian body lay ahead, and Powell wanted to view it closer. Portugee guessed at his motivation. Powell hadn't covered himself with glory this morning. The least he could do was to bring back the information who had done the raiding.

Portugee got down and toed the Indian over. That was more distortion on the face rather than agony. The Indian had died easier than Tillery.

"What is he, Portugee?"

Portugee squinted up at Powell from his squatting position. "Brûlé, I'd say, Captain." That didn't mean anything as to what the other raiders had been. All of those tribes were under one head now.

Powell nodded and wheeled his horse. This morning's loss gnawed on him hard.

Thoughts picked at Portugee as the wagon rumbled back toward the fort. Most enlisted men were buried in unmarked graves. Portugee wondered if the Army even knew the names of next of kin. He shrugged the thoughts away. That wasn't his problem.

He drove to the stable area, and more men gathered around the wagon. Death had a horrible fascination, particularly for men in the same trade. Portugee could guess at the thoughts behind those stolid faces. A man couldn't help but think, tomorrow and that could be me.

"Lawson, Givings, bury him," Powell ordered.

That was another hated detail, but nothing showed on the two men's faces. Somebody would probably say a few words over Tillery. Those words wouldn't mean much to anybody who heard them; certainly not Tillery.

He unhitched the mules and gave them some grain. They hadn't done much today to earn it, but he had a fondness for mules. They were a sensible, honest animal, and a man didn't have to be constantly on guard for the foolishness he could expect from a horse.

Powell and Hutson waited for him to finish. Powell must be staying around as long as he could to delay that report to Carrington.

"Are you going with us, Portugee?" Powell asked.

Portugee must have shown some surprise. He hadn't had any part in that raid.

"I thought you'd like to tell the colonel what they were."

"Sure," Portugee answered.

His face hardened at the sight of Fetterman approaching them. He wished Fetterman was wise enough to keep his mouth shut, but from his previous contact with him he would say the man had no caution in something like that.

Fetterman's eyes had a shine as though he was pleased about something. He ignored Hutson and Portugee. "Captain, you lost some horses, didn't you?"

That nettled Powell, and it showed. Hutson couldn't keep the hot youth out of his face.

"Would you have stopped it?" Powell demanded.

Fetterman gave him a cold, appraising glance. "I would have gone after the horses and gotten them back."

"Mr. Hutson!" Powell's sharp tone kept Hutson from speaking.

He swung his eyes back to Fetterman. "I think you would have, Captain. Without knowing what was in the trees."

He brushed by him, and Portugee and Hutson followed him. That had been rancor darkening Fetterman's face. He would not let Powell's remark go unpaid. Hutson would catch the brunt of it unless Powell's rank protected him.

They walked into Carrington's office, and the corporal said, "The colonel is waiting for you."

From the corporal's tone Portugee imagined Carrington had waited an impatient time.

Carrington stood behind his desk, and his face was unhappy. He didn't ignore Powell's and Hutson's salutes, Portugee decided as much as though he didn't see the salutes.

"What was the count, Captain?"

Powell's misery was in his voice. "Twenty-six horses lost, Colonel. Tillery was killed."

"Oh, my God." The words escaped Carrington's control. He was harassed by something too big for him. He sank wearily into his chair.

Powell's face burned. It was never pleasant to face criticism, even implied.

"Should I have gone after them, sir?" Fetterman's thrust had lodged hard.

Carrington looked at him with brooding eyes. "Did you know what was out there, Captain? Would it have been better to have nobody come back?"

Portugee thought he heard Powell's sigh of relief. The colonel was placing no blame on him.

Carrington looked at Portugee. "What were they, Portugee?"

"We looked at the dead Indian. I'd say Brûlé. But what the others were—" He let a shrug finish the sentence. It said he didn't get close enough to the others to see.

"Twenty-six horses." Carrington's words were barely audible. He wasn't talking to them. His haunted eyes looked at a frightening specter. "That makes us short of everything," he burst out. "Men, horses, and weapons. I've got to make Omaha see it."

Portugee was the only one who dared speak. "What does the colonel propose?"

Carrington didn't throw up his hands, but Portugee had the feeling he wanted to.

"Stop grazing the horses outside of the fort. We cannot afford to lose more of them."

Powell nodded. With the grazing shut off, it meant an immediate drain upon the hay stacks.

His face was wooden. "Yes, sir."

"Send me a rider. I have to get another dispatch through to Horseshoe Station."

Horseshoe Station was the nearest telegraph station, and its distance put a thinning in Powell's lips. But he replied evenly enough, "Yes, sir."

"I'll be ready in a half-hour. That's all." Carrington dismissed them.

Powell and Hutson saluted and wheeled. Portugee followed them out of the door.

The picture of Carrington's haggard face was vivid in Portugee's head. Outside he said, "I'd hate to be in the colonel's bind. How are you going to pick that rider?"

"I'm going to ask for a volunteer."

Portugee grimaced. He would hate to have to volunteer for that chore.

He and Bridger were there when Powell had the men lined up before him. Powell gave it to them straight and hard, making no effort to ease his words. "I need a volunteer to carry a dispatch to Horseshoe Station. I won't try to tell you it will be a simple job."

Portugee and Bridger exchanged glances. Powell had understated it.

Portugee saw the uneasy movement of men's eyes and the bobbing of Adam's apples.

"I wouldn't want it," Bridger muttered.

57

Portugee's hard cast of expression said he agreed with that. Not a man moved. Powell wasn't going to get his volunteer.

Sergeant Murphy looked on either side of him, and that could have been a curling of the thin line of his mouth. He stepped forward one pace.

"I volunteer, sir."

Powell had something else in his mind, but he didn't say it. "Report to Colonel Carrington in a half-hour." His tone and expression gave no indication of what he really felt. "You will leave after dark. Do you know the trail?"

"The captain remembers that I came up it, yesterday," Murphy murmured.

Powell's head bobbed. "I'll pick out a horse and have it saddled for you." He returned Murphy's salute before he turned.

Portugee watched Powell walk away. He wouldn't want the position of command.

"Will he get through?" Bridger asked.

It was the question looming big in everybody's mind. Portugee grunted. Bridger's guess was as good as his. His eyes were on Murphy. Nobody walked with him. His volunteering had already put him in the class of a lonely man.

"Powell's got a good man." He knew the source of his odd irritation. Was he already admitting Murphy's failure? He was not, he thought violently. It was just too damned bad that Murphy had to go on this.

It was after dark when he arrived at the water gate. Morbid curiosity had drawn quite a few people. A private held a saddled horse. It snorted, and its frosty breath made little white clouds.

Portugee thought that Powell had picked out the horse well. The bay gelding was a rangy, long-legged horse. If Murphy had a chance to break through, the gelding should outleg the Sioux ponies. He would not dwell on that big "if." Powell could have picked only one better; that would be the colonel's thoroughbred, Gray Eagle. That wasn't a choice Powell could make.

"Do you have your dispatch, Sergeant?" Powell asked.

Murphy patted an inner pocket. "Yes, sir."

Powell thrust out his hand. "Good luck, Sergeant."

The moving flame of a torch picked out Murphy's face. That might be a fleeting impression of a wry smile. "Sure," he said and swung into the saddle.

A private withdrew the bars from the gate, and the gelding trotted through it. The small sound of the hoofs was immediately lost in the wind. Powell stood with bowed head. Portugee wanted to offer him a drink and withheld it. Powell might want a drink, but he wouldn't want company. The goddamned waiting, Portugee thought in sudden fury. It's going to rack all of us.

He had to go back and stay with Hattie. He had earlier given her a brief résumé of what was going on, and even if he hadn't, she would know. Bad news couldn't be hushed, and it had an insidious way of traveling. He had eaten a meager supper, the heavy thoughts curbing his appetite. He was grateful that she didn't encroach upon them. Thank God. She wasn't the kind of a woman who needed talk for solace.

He walked into the cabin, and he couldn't answer the plea in her eyes. He simply didn't know what was going on out there now.

"He got off," he said.

That didn't tell her a thing. "Off" didn't mean getting through.

She didn't say the false words that Murphy would make the ride. Instead, she caught his hand, and its pressure was everything she could give him now.

"The kids in bed?"

She nodded. She had overcome their protests at going to bed at an early hour.

"I'll heat the coffee, John."

He shook his head. He tried to smile at her and wasn't

59

successful. The waiting was equally as hard on her. Any talk, around the fort tonight, would be hushed. The same thought would be on everybody's mind; how much time had passed, where was Murphy?

He wanted to pace about the cabin. That might ease him, but it would only increase her worry.

The sharp rattle of rifle fire jerked him out of the morass of his thoughts. Hattie had heard it too, for her eyes were strained, her breathing faster.

He would say a half-dozen shots were fired, then he heard two more. None of it was organized fire, and he would say all of those shots were wild, jerked out of a man in his desperation.

"It doesn't mean anything," he told Hattie.

He snatched up his rifle and ran outdoors, catching a glimpse of her face as he passed her. She didn't believe his lie.

This was the last night he would let Hattie and the kids stay in the cabin. He would have to get Carrington's permission to move inside the fort.

Fisher and Wheatley came running out of the other cabin and joined him. He shook his head before they could put their questions into words. He didn't know any more than they did what was happening.

The front gate was still closed, and sentries were clumped above it.

"We saw a rider, dashing for the gates, sir," a man called back to somebody on the ground. "He got almost here before he turned and whipped away. He left something out there."

Portugee turned and saw a huddled, shapeless mask, its whiteness showing up against the dark earth. He could name it without getting closer. Something tight gripped his throat, and his breathing was ragged.

He looked up, and a sentry peered over the wall at them. "It's Portugee," he called. "Fisher and Wheatley. We'll go out and see what it is." He led the way toward the shapeless mass.

He looked down at the sad remains of a brave man. A daring Sioux had dared come this far before he dumped the burden his party carried. It was a supreme taunt, and the helplessness of Portugee's rage choked him.

"Send out some men," he yelled.

He heard the squeaking of tortured hinges, and men poured out of it. Powell and Hutson were in the van, and Portugee waited for them before he said anything.

An irregular ring formed about Murphy's body. It lay face up, his features distorted by a hard dying. Portugee heard a small sound coming from Hutson, and it might have been a gagging.

Murphy had been stripped and mutilated, and his hands and feet were gone. Some swore, and others stood in stony silence. Portugee thought, two Sioux are wearing his uniform; one the coat, the other the pants with the front and back cut out of them. Oh God, if he only had those Sioux before him now.

"He didn't get very far," a private said.

It was one of the stupid remarks made under the stress of the time, but Portugee forgave him for it.

Powell's face was carved out of stone. Portugee could guess what the man felt inside. Murphy had volunteered to him.

"Bring him in," Powell said, and his voice sounded as though it had suddenly aged twenty years.

Portugee watched four men pick up the body and proceed toward the gates. His blood churned and boiled at the useless waste of it.

"What are you going to do now, Portugee?" Fisher asked.

"Move Hattie and the kids inside. Jim, you'd better do the same."

Wheatley nodded. "I guess it's past time, Portugee."

CHAPTER EIGHT

Lyford was doing a rushing business tonight. Every table was occupied, and men stood against the walls. Portugee knew the reason why Lyford was getting all of this trade. A man wanted to burn the thoughts out of his head with whiskey. Wasn't he trying to do the same thing?

He finished his glass and let the whiskey belt him again. But outside of that first authoritative wallop, it wasn't doing him any good. His thoughts were as clear as they always were.

The talking, the banter was missing tonight. When men spoke, it was in hushed tones. They were having the same trouble as Portugee; he couldn't get Murphy's burial out of his mind.

Hutson, Fisher, and Wheatley sat with him. Portugee didn't know where Powell was. He hadn't seen him since Powell had turned away from Murphy's grave.

Fisher and Wheatley stared blankly at nothing. The whiskey wasn't touching them either, but then it rarely did.

Hutson looked at the table top with brooding eyes. The whiskey was beginning to touch him. It showed in the increased color in his face, and when he spoke, his words weren't quite clear.

Let it touch him, Portugee thought. Let it blot out his thinking. Hutson had soldiered with Murphy at Laramie, and he had ridden up the trail with him. Some remembrances were riding him hard.

Portugee had seen Carrington at the burial and had exchanged brief words with him. Carrington's face had been a mask, expressing nothing. But he had stood as though his joints were fused, and nothing could bend them. Was he blaming himself for Murphy's death? If so, what was Powell's feeling? Powell had made the final selection.

Carrington had given permission, and Portugee and Wheatley had moved their families into the stockade. As undermanned as the fort was it hadn't been hard to find quarters. Neither of them had many possessions, and the move hadn't taken long. Portugee had tried to talk to Hattie, but the words wouldn't come easy. What could he promise her? There had been no accusation in her eyes, but he felt as though there should have been. His responsibility bore down upon him. He had made the choice of wintering here.

Fisher lifted his empty glass. "Another one?" He received nods all around the table.

Why not, Portugee thought gloomily.

Wheatley caught Kathy's eye and waved her over. She was trotting to keep up with the demand. This rush of business had to be putting a shine in Lyford's eyes.

Hutson's mind must be really full for he hadn't paid her too much attention since he came in here.

She passed Fetterman's table, and he caught her hand. With his other hand, he caressed her arm. Kathy jerked her arm away, and her eyes flashed. She had trouble controlling the words she wanted to say.

Fetterman threw back his head and laughed, and it was an alien sound in the room.

Hutson caught that for his head lifted, and he turned it toward the table.

It's just as well he didn't see Fetterman paw her, Portugee thought.

"Another round, Kathy," Wheatley said as she came up to the table.

She had long experience in seeing whiskey work on men, and she saw it in Hutson. "Tom, do you think you—" She bit her lips, chopping off what she intended to say.

64

Hutson's smile had a hard-set quality. "Have you got a reason why not, Kathy?"

If she had one, she didn't voice it.

They've made progress, Portugee thought. It's on a first-name basis now. He had an idle curiosity as to how many times Hutson had been in here by himself.

She took the empty glasses, and Hutson watched her walk away. She gave Fetterman's table a wide berth, going out of her usual course.

If Hutson noticed it, he didn't understand why. But Fetterman did for his laughter rang out again. If Fetterman wasn't drunk, he was rapidly approaching it. His talk was the loudest in the room, and his words were slurred. His eyes were getting that glassy shine.

Portugee's face turned sour. "Nothing seems to be bothering him."

"It should be," Hutson replied. "Murphy saved him from a war club. He cut that Sioux off of his pony before he could swing at Fetterman."

Portugee's eyes lighted with interest. He hadn't heard that before. Maybe he had misjudged Fetterman. Maybe he needed the whiskey as much as any other man in the room.

Kathy brought the drink, and Portugee only drank half of it. This room was suddenly oppressive, and it wasn't the thick layer of smoke or the subdued talk that caused it. Gloom was a pall on every man, and he had had enough of it.

He pushed back from the table and stood. "I've had enough of this." His eyes covered the others, and their expressions didn't agree with him.

"Tell my woman I won't be much longer," Wheatley said.

Portugee nodded and walked to the door. He took a deep breath of the still, colder air. Stars twinkled like bits of frozen ice. The fort was hushed, and only the occasional beat of sentries' boots on the walkways drifted to him. The gloom, back in that room, had been bad, and Portugee wondered why. A soldier's death was no new thing, but this last one had had a much greater impact. Was Murphy that popular, or his death put them squarely against a sharper reality, lessening hope? The latter, Portugee decided.

A dim light was in Powell's quarters as he passed it, and upon sudden impulse, Portugee turned and knocked on the door. He didn't think Powell was going to answer it, and he knocked again.

He heard the drag of Powell's feet as he crossed the room and opened the door.

"Yes?" There was no invitation in Powell's tone.

"Just wanted to talk to you, Captain."

Powell fought some indecision, then stepped aside for him to enter. "Sit down."

Portugee saw the bottle of whiskey on the small table. A filled glass was beside it. If that had been a full bottle to start with, Powell had done some hard drinking to lower its level that much.

Powell set another glass on the table and waved at the bottle.

Portugee grinned. "That don't do much good, Captain," he said softly. "I tried that route."

Powell gave him a savage flick of his eyes. "Do you know something better?"

"Not right now," Portugee confessed. Powell was punishing himself.

Powell sat down, staring at his long legs stretched out before him. He wouldn't admit it, but he needed somebody to talk to.

Portugee watched Powell empty the glass. "Have you talked to the colonel?"

Powell's eyes had a fierce gleam at some memory. "Most of the afternoon."

Here were two men who had faced reality for a long time. Its grinding was chewing both of them up fine. They had made a lot of talk but had found no solution. Powell showed it.

66

"He asked Jim Bridger to try and get through," Powell muttered.

Portugee didn't have to ask what Bridger had replied. Bridger wouldn't try it. Fisher and Wheatley weren't here, but he could speak for them.

"What's the answer, Captain?"

Powell emptied his glass before he spoke.

"Not a goddamned one." That last drink seemed to have thickened his speech.

Nothing Portugee could say would ease those bleak words. Laramie had men they could send, but Laramie wouldn't move unless Omaha ordered them. He felt a quick rage at a headquarters that refused to understand what was happening. God knew that Carrington had sent Omaha enough requests for help. Was it going to take the fort's destruction to make Cooke move?

"He was a good man," Powell muttered.

Powell wasn't speaking to him. Portugee didn't comment. Powell had spent time at Laramie. He had probably known Murphy there.

He reached for the bottle. "I think I will have a drink, Captain."

CHAPTER NINE

Hattie beat Portugee up in the morning. The good smell of coffee drifted to him, and he heard the sputtering of bacon in a frying pan.

He looked over at the kids, and they hadn't stirred yet. He grinned as he pulled on his clothes. They fought going to bed at night and fought getting out of it in the morning as equally hard. He wished he had the protective cloak given to children. Nothing real touched them. They worried about only the present moment. The next one was too far away to worry about.

Hattie had a cup of coffee for him when he approached the stove. Her attempt at a smile wasn't a success. Worry was the enemy of happiness, destroying any outward sign of it.

"I didn't sleep very much." It was a partial apology for his tardiness this morning.

She touched his hand as though in need of physical contact. "I know you didn't."

His restlessness was the cause of her not sleeping well. She always knew when he was disturbed.

"Do you have to work today, John?" Her voice didn't show any stress, but it was in her. She didn't want him to leave the walls today.

He smiled wryly. "Water and wood have to be brought in," he pointed out. That was no rebuke in his words. Maybe the routine of daily living was a good thing for a man. At least, keeping occupied was better than just sitting around with his thoughts.

She nodded her acquiescence, though that wasn't in her heart. She didn't say "be careful" though it might have been in her eyes. He appreciated that.

He tried to eat with his usual appetite, and that didn't fool her, either.

He pushed back his unfinished food. "Too much whiskey, last night. I always get in trouble when I don't take your advice."

That was another false excuse, and she knew it. She came to him with an unusual passion, and her arms went about him. They held him tight for a long moment, and he made no effort to avoid their clinging. It was a sad consolation for a woman.

She stepped back, not wanting him to know she had given away to the rush of her feelings.

He slipped into a sheepskin coat. If last night's nip was any indication, the morning would be colder than yesterday.

He shrugged. "The same old thing, I guess. Hauling water."

He picked up his rifle and tucked it under one arm. "I may be home a little early."

He opened the door and looked back. "One day at a time, Hattie. That's all we can do."

His last sight of her before the door closed was of her standing in the middle of the floor. How hard she worked to control her expression, but she couldn't do anything about her eyes.

He hadn't even heard reveille. It had to be over for men were streaming toward the mess hall.

He saw Powell and hurried his step to catch up with him. From the last he had seen of Powell the night before, for him to be up this early was quite a feat.

Powell looked like hell. His face was gaunt, and his eyes. He reminded Portugee of a wet piece of laundry that had been slapped too hard and too long against a rock. He wondered how Hutson looked this morning.

"Good morning, Captain."

Powell grimaced at the greeting. "I don't find it so. I suppose I made a damned fool of myself."

Portugee shook his head, smiling as he did. He didn't want Powell taking either the gesture or the smile as criticism. "Every now and then, a man needs a little help."

Powell scowled, refusing Portugee's easy explanation. "I haven't even got that excuse." He was a hard judge on himself. "How about breakfast?"

"I've already ate." If Powell felt as bad as he looked, his queasy stomach would refuse food.

"I just want coffee. Did I tell you that Colonel Carrington ordered the details accompanying wood and water wagons are to be doubled?"

"You didn't." It was welcome news to Portugee. The wood wagons would need it the most. They had to go farther to get wood. The water wagon wouldn't hardly be from under the fort's nose.

"I should have told you. That's what happens to a man when he makes a hog of himself with whiskey."

"Sure," Portugee said and turned away. Powell would berate himself until he felt better.

Wheatley and Fisher were at the stables when Portugee arrived. His eyebrows rose at the sight of them hitching teams to wagons.

"We're going out with the wood wagons," Wheatley said in disgust. Getting wood was hard work, and Wheatley detested anything connected with it. Fisher was a happy-go-lucky individual. He claimed a man had to put in so many hours a day; what he did didn't matter to him.

"Carrington's doubling the guard for the wagons," Portugee said.

Wheatley spat on the ground. "That's better." He was silent a moment as he adjusted harness and tightened buckles. "You left too early last night."

Fisher grinned at some memory. "For a little bit I thought we were going to have some excitement."

Portugee waited, then saw he was going to have to ask. "What happened?"

"Fetterman tried to paw Kathy again. Hutson jumped him hard. He said he'd knock his head off, if Fetterman touched her again." Fisher shook his head in regret. "It's too bad it was stopped."

Portugee compared Fetterman's size with Hutson's. Maybe Hutson was lucky that it was stopped. "Who stopped it?"

"Officers jumped in between them. Fetterman looked as though he was crazy when they dragged him away."

Portugee could imagine how those eyes looked. That would nail solidly the bad feeling between the two men. Carrington would explode, if he heard about it. He would hear, Portugee thought. Somebody would make sure he heard. Good Lord! Carrington had enough on his shoulders without his officers wrangling among themselves.

It wouldn't stop there. Fetterman would see to that. Hutson had scratched his ego, and Fetterman couldn't let it rest there.

His sympathies lay all with Hutson, but he held his remarks. Adding his little bit wouldn't help the matter. Should he say anything about it to Powell? He pushed the question away. It would get to Powell. Nothing was secret on an Army post. Besides, it wasn't any of his business.

He loaded the empty barrels into the wagon bed and tossed in the buckets. Water would be dipped out of the creek and passed along a chain of men until they were emptied into the barrels. It was a cold, wet business for a man couldn't help but get water splashed on him.

He had time for a smoke before the detail straggled up. They would be reluctant to go outside the walls today, and after yesterday, he couldn't blame them. He could be certain of one thing. Not a man out there would be half asleep on his job.

He let the wood wagons precede him out of the main gates. That was the more dangerous job; they had farther to go. He lifted his hand to Fisher and Wheatley and turned toward

72

the creek. It was still running, but ice had crept farther out from the banks. It would take the most severe freezing to stop running water, and even then it usually broke out in isolated spots. He hated the ice when it got thick. Chopping through it was hard, frustrating work.

He let the soldiers hand-pass the buckets to the wagon where they were emptied. The private, dumping the buckets into the barrels, was wet from his knees down, before the first barrel was half-filled.

Portugee sat on the seat, his eyes searching the country. It seemed peaceful enough. At this moment, a man could swear not an Indian was around. He hadn't better count on it, he thought. He looked back at the walls. He wouldn't be so cocky, if they hadn't been so near. Every man, on the detail, got the same feeling of security when he looked at those walls.

He was glad when the last barrel was filled. The day's work wasn't over, but this much was behind him. He kept the team to a walk and listened to a familiar noise; the creaking of the wagon bed, the squeaking of its wheels and the sloshing of the water in the barrels. The squeaking put a frown on his face. Those wheels would have to be greased.

He had to leave the barrels at various spots, around the fort, and he stopped at each one, while the barrels were unloaded. He didn't get down to help. That wasn't part of his job, and the soldiers had enough muscle to manhandle the heavy barrels out of the wagon bed. They grunted or swore, and a tiny smile flicked across Portugee's lips. Neither of those things helped any, but he was for it, if a man thought it did. The stables would take a full load. Horses and mules required a lot of water. It would be a long day before they were through. Tomorrow would start another day just like this one. Portugee grimaced. What was it that he had told Hattie about getting through life; a day at a time.

"That does it," he said as the last load was deposited. He watched the detail plod away, their shoulders sagging. Every man of them had earned his weariness.

73

He unhitched the teams and gave them a feed of grain. He frowned at the level in the granary. It caused no immediate concern, but what of the days ahead? He shook his head. A man couldn't help but worry about the future.

He started to leave the stables when he saw Kathy across the way. She bent against the wind, and it whipped at her skirts. He grinned in appreciation. The wind could do some interesting things with a woman's skirts.

Fetterman came around a corner, and his face brightened at the sight of her. He blocked her way, and Portugee's eyes hardened. The damned fool wouldn't learn.

Kathy tried to step around him, and Fetterman moved to check her. She stepped back, and a wall stopped her. Portugee was too far away to hear what was said, but something passed between them, for her head lifted, and she stared at the captain.

Fetterman moved quickly, and his arms went on either side of her, his hands going against the wall and pinning her.

Portugee swore in his throat. Somebody was going to have to break that up.

He took a step and stopped. Hutson was coming this way. He wouldn't stand for that.

Portugee picked up his stride again, and he wasn't sure what he was going to do. He was close enough to hear Hutson say, "Let her go. I told you before to leave her alone." His voice crackled with anger.

That hard shine was in Fetterman's eyes again. "You're mixed up, aren't you, Mr. Hutson? You can't tell me anything."

Maybe it was his rank talking, or just plain hardheadedness. Portugee would choose the latter. Kathy was pressed against the wall, her eyes round, the knuckles of one hand pressed against her lips.

"Tom, let go. It doesn't matter."

She could say that, but Hutson couldn't. His face was livid with anger, and he was as tight as a bowstring. Portugee wasn't sure what he was going to do. He might be able to stop it, but Hutson's rage would make him hard to control.

He shook his head, motioning Kathy to make no further protest. It had to come sometime; it might as well be now. He looked around and saw nobody else. No one was around to step in between them this time.

"I won't tell you again," Hutson snapped.

Fetterman's taunting look was a whip, lashing Hutson. His tone was worse. "What will you do, Mr. Hutson?"

Hutson's fury ran his words together. "If you weren't wearing that coat—"

Fetterman started unbuttoning his coat. "Are these bars worrying you? Why, that can be fixed in a hurry."

Hit him, Portugee begged. If you are going to do it, get in the first lick. That first blow always carried a telling weight.

It was already planted in Hutson's head. He took a long, forward step, and he had good momentum behind his fist. He caught Fetterman flush in the face, and Fetterman was rocked back a broken step. He tried to retain his balance, but that blow had loosened his legs. They went limber on him, and he fell.

Kathy moaned and shut her eyes.

That won't stop him, either, Portugee thought. Fetterman sat on the ground, his eyes glazed, his face slack. A trickle of blood ran from his nose. It filled Portugee with an immense satisfaction. Hutson looked slender beside Fetterman's bulk, but whatever happened, he had drawn the first blood.

"Get up," Hutson begged.

Portugee grinned. Hutson was a feisty rooster, and nothing would get the taste of blood out of his mouth.

Fetterman shook his head to clear his eyes, and he finished unbuttoning his coat. "Why, I intend to," he murmured. "I wouldn't disappoint you." He struggled out of his coat and let it fall on the ground.

He's tough enough, Portugee admitted. A solid punch,

75

like the last one he caught, took something out of a lot of men.

Hutson was on him before Fetterman fully got his feet under him. Fetterman backed, and he had clever arms. They picked off most of Hutson's blows. It's too bad, Portugee thought, that Hutson's got more fury instead of skill. Already, Hutson's breathing had a rasping, sobbing sound. He was spending himself with wild exertion, and he put no thinking behind it.

He didn't see Fetterman's blow that dropped Hutson, but Hutson was on his back, his mouth loose, his eyes blinking bewilderedly.

Portugee didn't look at Kathy as a little shriek was torn from her.

It was too bad, but Fetterman was in control now. He stood easy, an amused smile on his face. "Doesn't that convince you now, Mr. Hutson?"

It didn't. Hutson blew out a ragged breath and scrambled to his feet. He made another mistake. Instead of waiting to be sure all of his facilities were back, he rushed in again.

Fetterman parried the wild swings and dug a fist deep into Hutson's belly. Portugee winced at the explosive burst of Hutson's breath. That one had hurt.

Hutson doubled over, his arms wrapped around his belly. Fetterman landed on his exposed jaw. It straightened up Hutson, and he fell over backward. His legs buckled, and he landed on his back again.

"Stop it," Kathy moaned.

Portugee shook his head at her. Maybe he should step in and stop it, but Hutson wasn't done yet. No man had a claim to take any feeble chance that was left in Hutson. He bled from the mouth, and his movements were uncoordinated, but he was trying to get up. His arms were too limber to lift his body, but he kept making the effort. He shook his head to get the dizziness out of it, and every time he did, droplets of blood flew. Portugee knew what he was up against for he had been in such a spot before. Hutson had a lot to overcome. He had weakness and nausea and hurt to contend with, and from what he did from now was the mark of a man.

Disappointment grew in Portugee. Hutson wasn't going to make it.

That malicious grin was plastered on Fetterman's face. "They slighted your education at the Point, Mr. Hutson. They didn't teach you the rudiments of how to defend yourself."

Portugee hated a mouth fighter, particularly when he was winning. But Fetterman's words were the goad Hutson needed.

It took tremendous effort for him to get to his knees, and his mouth had twisted from the strain of it. He wavered back and forth, and he hung there, his treacherous legs refusing to lift him farther.

He can't go any farther, Portugee thought dismally. It's over.

He underestimated how brightly the last spark in Hutson glowed. Fetterman didn't see it, either. He was too sure of himself, and he stood too close.

Hutson dived from his knees and struck Fetterman's thighs with his shoulders. His arms clamped around them, and his momentum carried Fetterman over onto his back.

This new contact must have fed that spark for Hutson fought like a crazed wildcat, and that was always a difficult animal to bag.

Portugee wanted to whoop his delight, and he remembered Kathy in time to stop it. She wasn't delighted. Her face was more stricken than ever.

Hutson had only determination in place of skill, and for a moment, Portugee thought it might be enough. Fetterman tried to knock him off, and Hutson was too close to him for his blows to have much effect, or maybe Hutson didn't even feel them. Fetterman tried to roll him off, and Hutson clung like a leech. Every time Fetterman rolled over Hutson came up on top. He fought like an enraged kid, using everything he had. His arms flailed like a windmill running under a

77

strong wind, and he butted with his head and tried to slam his knees into him.

He hurt Fetterman. It showed in his dirty face with the bloodstains on it. It showed in his open, gasping mouth. A man grew frantic under punishment like that and could go all to pieces, but Fetterman was tougher than that. He waited for the right moment, and his timing was precise. He jabbed his elbow into Hutson's throat. Hutson's head flew back, and Portugee heard him gag.

The opportunity was all that Fetterman needed. He used his strength and threw Hutson off of him. He was still frantic and it showed in his animal-like scramblings to put distance between him and Hutson for enough time to get to his feet.

Hutson was much slower, and he had too much trouble with his breathing. He dug at his throat as though he was trying to open it to the air.

He won't make it again, Portugee thought with sadness.

He turned his head at the pounding of feet. A dozen men ran this way, drawn by the activity. Powell led them, and Portugee checked his impulse. Let Powell stop it.

He looked back, and Fetterman ran at the man, on the ground, driven perhaps by his fear of losing. He drew back one leg and drove the toe of the boot into Hutson's body. The force was enough to jolt him several feet along the ground.

Portugee's eyes blazed, but Powell was running by him. Powell drove his shoulder into Fetterman and knocked him backward. Fetterman made a half-dozen broken strides before he could regain his balance. He caught it, and his arms went up in defense.

Powell's mask of rage invited him to make an objection. Sanity untwisted Fetterman's face, and Powell's size and fury registered on him. His arms dropped, and he tried to say it easily, but his pumping lungs wouldn't let him do that.

"Just a personel argument, Captain. It's over now."

Powell stared at him with cold dislike. "It takes a kicking, does it?"

Fetterman looked around at the awed faces and pulled his tattered dignity about him. "It's not your fight, Captain," he said sullenly.

Kathy was down on her knees in the dust, and she sobbed as she lifted Hutson's head. She soiled her handkerchief with dirt and blood as she dabbed at his face.

Powell didn't have to ask what had happened. He had seen the beginning of this quarrel in Lyford's place, and an awareness of its development was in his face. He whirled with sudden violence and yelled at the men, "Break it up. There's nothing here for you." He took a threatening step. "I'll court-martial every man who doesn't move."

They broke and scattered before the sweep of his authority and cold anger. They shuffled away, throwing glances over their shoulders. They would have a new subject of conversation tonight.

Powell turned back to Fetterman. "That includes you, too, Captain."

Portugee saw a flash of alarm in Fetterman's eyes, then it was hidden. That disdainful twist was back on his lips.

"Ask him who started it, Captain."

"I will," Powell said grimly. "The colonel will expect to see you in his office after supper."

The alarm flashed in Fetterman's eyes again. He sought for words and couldn't find them. He reached down, picked up his coat, and slapped it against his leg. He stalked away without looking back.

"Did you see it all, Portugee?" That harsh tone was still with Powell.

"From the beginning, Captain. Fetterman hasn't learned to keep his hands off of her."

Powell's eyes swept to Kathy and Hutson, but he was still listening. Hutson sat up, but his head was drooping, and Kathy was supporting him. His breathing sounded easier.

"Go on," Powell said.

"Hutson came up in time to see Fetterman stopping her, and he didn't like the way he did it. He called him hard. He

79

was aware he was up against a captain, for he begged him to take off his coat." A hard flicker of amusement was on his lips. "He was doing all right until Fetterman jammed his elbow into his throat. That took it out of him."

Powell surveyed Hutson's battered face. "It looks like Fetterman didn't leave him a thing. You be at the colonel's office, too."

That must have startled Portugee, for Powell snapped, "You're the only one who saw it all."

Portugee grinned. Powell wasn't counting at all on Kathy's witnessing. A woman could get pretty flighty under conditions like this.

"Are you telling Hutson too?"

Powell looked at Hutson again. "He'll be there." He added in a softer vein, "If he's able."

CHAPTER TEN

Both Fetterman and Hutson showed the marks of their fight, but Hutson was in far the worse shape. Each movement seemed to be painful for him, and the bruises on his face were taking on vivid color. They stood ramrod straight before Carrington, and their eyes were fixed on the wall, behind him.

Portugee had never seen an angrier man than the colonel. It was in his blazing eyes, in the tight line of his mouth. Carrington hadn't said anything yet, but every man in his office waited for the explosion they knew was coming. Even Powell waited uneasily, and he knew that Carrington's anger wouldn't be directed at him.

Portugee understood Powell's feeling. The atmosphere in the room had a frigid air, and he didn't take his usual chair.

"Captain Fetterman and Mr. Hutson reporting as directed, sir," Powell said.

"Of all the disgraceful—" Carrington had good control for he chopped off the rest of his words. "Go ahead, Captain Powell," he said coldly.

"They were fighting, sir. On the post."

Those blazing eyes rested on him. Carrington already knew that. He wanted to know why the fight. He waited, but Powell was going to have to be prompted. "You saw it, Captain?"

"Just the last few seconds of it. Mr. Hutson was on the ground. Captain Fetterman kicked him."

Carrington's eyes raked Fetterman. Portugee was damned

glad he wasn't in Fetterman's boots. Fetterman was a smart man; he kept his mouth shut.

"Who did see it?"

"Portugee—" Powell amended that hastily. "Mr. Phillips did, sir."

Portugee came under the impact of those eyes, and he hunted for the proper words to start.

"I was there from the start," he admitted.

"Go ahead," Carrington said in that frozen voice.

Portugee sighed. He had better tell it straight without trying to embellish it. "Captain Fetterman stopped Kathy. She didn't want to talk to him."

"Your guess, Mr. Phillips?"

"No, sir," Portugee said doggedly. "She showed it. Every time she tried to get away from him, he blocked her way. Then he pinned her against a wall."

Hutson couldn't hold his seething words any longer. "He was always doing it, sir. She had asked him before to let her alone. But he had to press his attention on her."

"Did I ask you to speak, Mr. Hutson?"

A dull wave of color flooded Hutson's face. "No, sir."

"Then don't."

Portugee got a glimpse of Hutson's rigid jaws. He was suffering more than just physically.

"Go on, Mr. Phillips."

"Mr. Hutson saw him and jumped him. He yelled for Captain Fetterman to keep his damned hands off her. Captain Fetterman asked him who he thought he was talking to. Mr. Hutson said take off his coat, and he'd show him." Portugee hesitated. The next would be the hardest to say, for Hutson had started it.

"I'm waiting," Carrington reminded him.

Portugee shrugged. "Then he hit him, sir."

"This is the most disgraceful thing I've ever heard of," Carrington exploded. "With everything facing us, my officers have time to fight among themselves. If I could safely send you back, both of you would be on your way to Laramie tonight."

"May I say something, Colonel?" Fetterman asked.

"You may not," Carrington snapped. "You haven't described the fight, Mr. Phillips."

Portugee couldn't completely check his grin. "He knocked the captain down. The captain got up, and he really hit Mr. Hutson. It put Mr. Hutson down, and I didn't think he could get up, but he did. The captain wasn't content to leave Mr. Hutson lying on the ground. He taunted him. It kinda prodded Mr. Hutson into getting back up."

"I'd like to hear what he said, Mr. Phillips."

"He asked if the Point hadn't taught him to protect himself. It drove Mr. Hutson crazy. It almost turned it."

Fetterman's breathing had a harsh rasp, and the color was in his face now.

Portugee wished he could read the thoughts behind Carrington's face. But nobody could probe those flinty eyes.

"Mr. Hutson didn't have much skill, sir. But he gave a pretty good account of himself. Until the captain jabbed his elbow into Mr. Hutson's throat. That jarred him loose. Mr. Hutson was still on the ground when the captain kicked him." Portugee lifted his hands and let them fall. "Captain Powell came up then."

Anger blazed from Carrington's eyes as he faced Fetterman and Hutson. "You two can thank your God you're not facing a court-martial. I can't afford to lose another man from my command. But you are confined to your quarters for one week."

They're lucky to be getting off with that, Portugee thought, but Fetterman couldn't let it alone.

"Will it be a matter of record, sir?"

"It will go on your records."

That caused Fetterman anguish; he couldn't keep it off of his face.

"From now on, you will avoid the young woman. If I hear

again—" Carrington did not have to say the rest. Fetterman knew it was no idle threat.

Portugee didn't hear Hutson sigh, but he was sure he did. The old man must remember his younger days. Carrington did not warn Hutson to stay away from Kathy.

"Dismissed," Carrington barked.

He took their salutes, and they wheeled and marched out of the office.

Carrington did not speak until the door closed on them. "Mr. Hutson walks stiffly. Was he hurt?"

"He got a pretty good boot in the ribs, Colonel," Portugee said. "I guess he feels it."

"See that the post surgeon checks it, Captain."

Powell felt relief too, at the way it had gone, for a faint smile was on his mouth. "I will, sir."

Carrington could take off that hard mask. "I would have thought the threat of the Sioux would fill a man's mind so full he wouldn't think of anything else."

Portugee grinned. "Not the young, Colonel. Maybe they are lucky to be able to think about something else.

Carrington grunted, but there was no particular displeasure in the sound. "Thank you, gentlemen."

It was another form of dismissal, but Portugee had one other thing to say. "I'll say you've got one hell of an officer."

He didn't speak the name, but Carrington understood. "I think so too, Mr. Phillips."

Portugee nodded. Both of them were speaking of the same man.

Outside, he said, "That came off better than I hoped for."

"Fetterman can thank the Sioux for one thing," Powell said savagely. "If the Sioux threat wasn't there, he could have been kicked out of the Army. I've seen less provocation get a man more punishment."

Portugee shrugged. He was a little tired of hearing about Fetterman. He walked a few steps in silence. "I think Kathy ought to know how it turned out."

84

"You tell her." Powell sounded as though he would just as soon be entirely rid of the matter.

Portugee smiled. "I hope Hutson doesn't hear about me talking to her and jump me for it. I saw him work on Fetterman. He's a tough one."

That wrung a small chuckle from Powell. "I'll tell him you're harmless. I'm going to tell him to report to the surgeon for a checkup."

Portugee watched him walk away. Powell might not have wanted his part in this, but Fetterman would never forgive him for it. Hell, he won't forgive Hutson or me, he thought.

Kathy saw him the moment he came into the room. She rushed up to him, and some inner urgency made her sound breathless. "Is he hurt bad, Portugee?"

"Only a little battered around the edges. The colonel just finished talking to him."

That put apprehension in her. "Did he blame him?"

"Some," Portugee admitted. "He ordered both of them to their quarters for a week."

"That isn't fair," she cried. "He was only—"

"Looking out for you," he interrupted. "The colonel took that into consideration. But Hutson did start it. Carrington had to give them equal punishment. He told Fetterman not to bother you again. He didn't tell Hutson that."

He watched with interest the warm flush of her face. "A week isn't a lifetime, Kathy."

He left her, feeling good. Even in this fear-ridden fort a man could find a few warm, rich moments. He had something to tell Hattie that wouldn't have its bleak overtones. A woman liked to live in a romance, even if it was happening to somebody else.

CHAPTER ELEVEN

A couple of minutes of light was chopped off of each day, and they crept into December. The cold steadily increased, and twice the winds brought in howling snowstorms. It was going to be a hard winter; Portugee could feel it in his bones. He didn't curse the weather too much, even though it made the chores of existence that much harder. Bad weather might work on their side. It could hold the Sioux close to their winter lodges.

That was the only hope for the Sioux hadn't gone. Their campfires still ringed the fort at night. Even a snowstorm that obscured those fires didn't make a man feel any easier. They were still out there.

Omaha thought that Carrington should take advantage of the winter; attack the Sioux and drive them from their shelter. That could have been wild exaggeration for Portugee knew how rumor could swell what was originally said. But the last report was that Carrington had been ordered by General Cooke to do just that. If it was true, Portugee cursed Cooke. He would like to see the general sit in just such a position. He would like Cooke to work his way out of it.

It was snowing again when Portugee walked into Lyford's. He felt the wetness of the flakes against his cheeks, and he couldn't see the sentries on the walls because of the white curtain. He should have worn his buffalo coat; it was warmer than his sheepskin.

Inside the door, he shook the snow off of his shoulders. The room was warm and lighted. Men crowded into here every time duty let them, and it wasn't hard to understand. A man could create an illusion of gaiety in here.

Fetterman and Hutson had been released from their quarters several days ago, and both of them were here tonight. But they kept carefully separated. They sat at tables on opposite sides of the room. It had quieted Fetterman down, but he hadn't forgotten it. It showed in the cold set of his eyes and in his frozen face. He wasn't talking much, and when he did, his words didn't carry far.

Portugee would take that. It was better than the other nights.

Kathy passed close to Fetterman's table, and Fetterman appeared not to even notice her. It tickled Portugee. At least, Fetterman had learned that much.

It hadn't lost Fetterman any standing with some of the officers; the usual ones were at his table. Mr. Grummond was there, and Portugee was sorry about that. He had thought Grummond would be smarter than that. Rank must be filling his eyes, or he was impressed by Fetterman's exploits.

Portugee looked about the room. Hutson and Kathy sat at a table, their heads close together. That caused a mild wonder in Portugee. He expected Lyford to be yelling at her to take care of business, but Lyford was beaming whenever he looked at them. Portugee's interest sharpened. Something must be decided between those two.

Powell was sitting by himself, and Portugee joined him. Powell had a gray brooding in him, and it was more than just the ordinary strain.

Portugee sat down. "Jim and Isaac been in yet?"

"Haven't seen them." It didn't look as though Powell would say what was on his mind.

Portugee jerked his head toward Hutson and Kathy. "At least, we've got a happy two people in here."

Powell looked at them and grunted. Portugee couldn't tell whether or not it was approval. Something more than drink was putting this heavy mood in Powell.

Kathy and Hutson rose and came toward them. Hutson

had that sheepish grin that a man gets on his face at certain times, and Kathy looked radiant. Portugee didn't need for them to tell him anything. It was written all over their faces. He put another glance on Powell. Surely, the man wasn't jealous.

"You tell them, Kathy," Hutson said. He looked more boyish than ever.

Kathy's words tumbled out and ran together. "We're engaged."

It had happened pretty fast, but at times like this, a man ran at things in fear that he could never get his hands on them. Portugee saw no ring on her finger. But where would a man find a ring in a besieged fort?

He sprang to his feet and wrung Hutson's hand. "I couldn't hear anything that would please me more." He pressed Kathy's hands. He was inwardly tight as he waited for Powell's reaction. He hoped Powell would say or show nothing that would spoil this moment for them.

Powell stood, and he said, "I'm glad." He shook Hutson's hand and gave Kathy his best wishes.

"This calls for a drink," Powell said.

Both of them declined it. Hutson didn't need a drink to make him taller than a tree, and Kathy's happiness didn't need a boost.

Powell didn't offer them a chair. "You two would rather be alone, wouldn't you?"

They exchanged a look, and they would. Portugee watched them back to their table. Fetterman hadn't missed that little byplay. His eyes were glittering.

Powell sat quietly in his chair, and Portugee didn't think he was going to speak again. Then Powell said, "Colonel Carrington sent out another dispatch rider tonight." His low voice wouldn't carry beyond the table.

Portugee remembered the fires in the hills. That ring of Sioux hadn't been broken. "Oh, goddamn it," he exploded.

Powell flashed him a savage look. "What else can the colonel do? Corporal Rymar has carried a dispatch before."

Portugee's face was stubborn. "Not lately, he hasn't." Powell was getting angry at Portugee's criticism, and he didn't give a damn.

"Colonel Carrington waited for another snow fall. Don't you think Rymar will get through?"

"No," Portugee said flatly. So this was the reason for Powell's gray brooding. "You don't, either."

That sigh was torn out of Powell's bowels. "What else could he do?"

Portugee ignored the plea in Powell's voice. "Maybe nothing else, I guess. But a man can bleed to death a drop at a time, if it goes on long enough. How long ago did Rymar leave?" he asked abruptly.

"About an hour. We stood there and listened a long time. We didn't hear anything."

Portugee's face was savage with anger. "How far do you think sound will carry against this wind?"

He stood, and Powell asked, "Where are you going?"

"The Sioux will bring him back." Powell could go to the walls or stay. Portugee didn't give a damn. "Just like they did Murphy."

A gray sickness wiped out the color in Powell's face. "I'm going with you."

"Suit yourself," Portugee said harshly.

He took a position on the walkway just beside the main gate. Right out there was where the Sioux had dumped Murphy's body. Powell stood beside him, trying to see through the snow. Some of Portugee's bitter criticism of him faded. Powell had had no more choice in this than Rymar had had. If a blame had to be fixed, it had to be placed on Carrington. And maybe he didn't have any more choice, either.

"I hope I'm wrong," Portugee muttered. He wore his buffalo coat, and it felt good. The cold bit deep at a man in a hurry.

Powell nodded. He was on the same rack that tortured all of them.

Portugee had no idea of how long they had been waiting.

The snow fell in slanting lines, and a man couldn't keep his face turned to it too long. Even when he looked into it, he couldn't see very far. A numbness crept along his hands and feet, and he took his hands out of his pockets and blew on them. If he got a shot, he didn't want gloves hampering his hands.

How long had they been out here? It seemed like an eternity. Hope kept wrestling with logic, and the logic won out. The time elapsed didn't mean anything, Portugee kept telling himself. Rymar had gotten a little farther than Murphy. That was all.

His rage was a steady flame. All he wanted was a chance of stopping the brave that brought Rymar back. He couldn't have that brave boasting of his bravery, while the others lauded him.

He started to say something to Powell and tensed. Had he heard some sound? He turned his head to ask Powell if he heard it too, and whipped it back. That was something he heard, and he strained facilities to see and hear. He caught the faint sound; that was the hard pound of running hoofs.

The wind whipped water into his eyes, and he could see nothing in that gray wall. The metal of the rifle felt frozen against his hands, and it was biting deeper.

He was beginning to believe that his senses were tricking him when he saw something black loom up against the falling snow, then the bobbing motion of a running horse burst out of the veil of snow.

He waited an instant until he was sure it was no trooper, trying to make the fort. That was an Indian pony, and no trooper rode it.

"Now," he yelled.

He heard the bark of Powell's rifle, and the horse didn't stop nor swerve. Powell cursed as he reloaded. An angry thought blossomed in the back of Portugee's head. Powell had brought an old Springfield with him. He could, at least, have picked up one of the cavalrymen's seven-shot Spencer.

Even that didn't come close to comparing with the newer, sixteen-shot repeating Henry.

Portugee tracked the pony in his sights and waited. A futile thought was in his head; he wished he had brought Wheatley and Isaac out here with him. They had Henrys, too. A running horse was a difficult target under such conditions. Two more Henrys would make it that more certain that Sioux did not ride away.

He squeezed the trigger and felt the dull jolt of the butt against his shoulder. He fired again and again, letting neither haste nor frustration rush him into frenzied shooting. He would know how successful he was when that horse went down.

He thought he saw the outline of feathers above the Sioux's head, and now he could see that the Indian drove a burdened pony toward the gates.

He squeezed the trigger once more, and the pony went down, sending two bodies flying from it. Portugee hadn't wanted to hit that pony; he wanted the rider.

The horse scrambled to its feet and whipped back into the curtain of snow. Portugee waited until the thud of its hoofs could no longer be heard. Neither of the forms, on the ground, had moved.

He looked at Powell, and his grin was like an animal's snarl. "That's one more of the bastards who won't get back."

CHAPTER TWELVE

Men did the assigned work, but a heavy hand of fear was crushing the spirit out of them. The question was seldom voiced, but it was in every eye. When is help coming?

Portugee wished he could answer that. He and Fisher and Wheatley had wrangled over the matter for too many hours.

"It isn't coming," Portugee said flatly.

Wheatley and Fisher were of a more optimistic vein. "It's got to come," they argued.

"How can it?" That was Portugee's stock answer. "No rider got through to tell them we need it."

"That's got to tell them something," Wheatley said stubbornly. "Any day, they'll be sending somebody up the trail to see what's happening up here."

That might be logical reasoning, Portugee thought, but it didn't fit the military mind. He had watched it work, and its reasoning was awesome. The chain of command was formed with ponderous links, and each demanded its proper time and attention. No officer dared do anything as drastic as moving troops unless it was approved by higher authority. He made a weak amendment to that. A dire emergency could force a lesser commander into action without waiting for permission from headquarters. How many sleepless hours had he struggled with a problem that had no solution? It had only two answers, and both of them were weak. The weather had to hold the Sioux to their lodges, or a rider had to get through to Laramie. Portugee didn't give the latter much consideration. That had been tried too many times already.

Wheatley started to say something and broke into a deep, shaking cough. It sounded as though his lungs were rattling against each other.

Portugee scowled at him. Both Fisher and Wheatley had colds, and continued exposure would only make both of their colds worse. Fisher had a runny nose that he couldn't seem to stop. This was part of the attrition that Carrington feared. It pared relentlessly at his strength without him taking a step outside the walls. The Sioux didn't have to attack. The onslaught of winter pounded at Carrington without the Sioux lifting a finger. The sick list grew steadily longer. Men hacked and spit, trying to free the phlegm from their lungs. Fever heated their faces and weakened their bones. They dragged around as though each foot weighed a hundred pounds. Portugee wouldn't doubt that a full third of the post was incapacitated to one degree or another.

"Neither of you are going out tomorrow," he stated. "Hattie's good at treating a cold. She's got some bear grease that she'll heat and smear on you."

Wheatley grimaced. He had been through that treatment before. The memory of its stickiness was in his grimace. But he didn't protest too much. Fort Phil Kearny didn't need the services of scouts any more. Fort Phil Kearny was on the defensive.

Fisher put up a weak argument. "Who's going to take our place?"

Portugee knew what was behind that question. The wood chore went on daily for the increasing cold consumed an appalling amount of fuel.

"I'll take one of the wagons," he said. "I can find somebody else to drive the others." He couldn't make his grin as firm as he wanted it. "My job's getting easier. We can go a day without getting more water." He had half-counted on taking a day off, but he let go of that without complaint. The cold did one favorable thing; it cut down the consumption of water for both human and animal need.

"Stay away from Lyford's tonight," he ordered. "If a man

isn't sick, that whiskey will make him so." He pushed back from the table and stood. "I'll tell Hattie to expect both of you."

He walked out of Wheatley's quarters. The snow was ankle-deep, but it hadn't fallen any more all day, and that was something in this country. He had seen some winters where it seemed as though it didn't miss snowing a single day.

He hadn't attended Rymar's funeral this morning, but he knew that burial detail had had hell, hacking through the frozen ground. If the frost line kept growing deeper in the ground, some of the burials would have to be put off until spring.

He squinted at the sky, and its frozen stars seemed larger and more vivid than a summer's. He hoped the weather would hold. More snow would only make tomorrow that much more difficult. A man prized each favorable day that he was given in a winter.

He guessed he had better tell Powell about the change in drivers. He grinned with no mirth. That was one advantage of a civilian job with the government. He could take off whenever he felt like it. A soldier never had that choice.

The wagons were hitched up and ready to go, and none of the accompanying detail were here. Portugee fidgeted on his seat. How long did they expect a man to wait in this cold?

Powell appeared, and his expression disapproved of something. He hadn't protested the change in drivers last night, and Powell wondered if something had changed his mind.

"Colonel Carrington is sending out forty men," he said curtly.

Portugee didn't find anything wrong with that, but he didn't speak. Something else was disturbing Powell.

"Captain Fetterman is commanding the detail." Powell watched Portugee's face. He read it correctly, for he said, "I don't like it any better than you do."

"I thought you were taking it out."

"So did I," Powell snapped. "Fetterman pleaded well with the colonel."

Both men were occupied with the same thought. Inactivity had fretted Fetterman. Portugee could almost look into the man's head. Fetterman had a blot on his record, and inactivity wouldn't erase it.

Portugee sighed. He was borrowing trouble. The wood wagons would be under the eye of Pilot Hill. The fort would be signaled the minute they were in trouble.

"Sure," he said woodenly. The clatter of hoofs stopped anything else he might want to say.

Fetterman rode up with the detail and lined them on each side of the wagons. Portugee's irritation rose. Why did Fetterman have to do everything with such a dash? Lieutenant Grummond was the only other officer, and Portugee frowned at him. Grummond was sold on the captain. It showed in his manner and actions. Portugee pushed away the irritation. Grummond was a grown man. He could make his own choices.

That thought led to another. He had seen Mrs. Grummond since the morning she had rescued his daughter, but only briefly and not more than long enough to exchange a few words. He was sorry for the neglect, but he had let the demands of the day pick the easier path for him.

Fetterman stood in his stirrups and swept his arm down. "Forward, ho."

Portugee picked up the reins and put the mules into motion. Fetterman had the voice for orders, Portugee thought sourly. Nobody on the fort could have missed hearing that.

He sat loosely on the wagon seat, letting his body give to the bumping and jolting of the wheels. The creaking of the wheels had lessened. Somebody had seen to his report that the wheels needed greasing.

He glanced every now and then at Fetterman. The man made quite a figure in a saddle, he admitted. He had all of the requirements to be an excellent officer; except that he was so damned hardheaded.

The train dropped over a rise that hid them from the fort, and an uneasiness rose in Portugee. He supposed he would feel it until he drove back into the fort. He shook his head. He had told Hattie "to take a day at a time," and here he was trying to hurry one along.

He was amazed to see how far they had cut into the woods. A day's cutting made no impression on a forest, but string a lot of them together, and a man could cut quite a hole in it.

A driver didn't have to do anything but sit and wait, but Portugee knew he was going to swing an ax. He enjoyed doing it. It occupied the time, and it kept the cold from biting into him.

He left his buffalo coat on the seat. The cold would creep through his lighter jacket, but a few minutes of exertion would chase it away.

He felt the edge of the ax and grunted approval. It was sharp. Nothing could wear out a man's muscles quicker than a dull edge.

He picked an eight-inch pine, and the chips flew. He had rhythm with power behind it enough to keep a constant stream of chips flying. He didn't look up until the tree fell. He noted with satisfaction that his tree was the first down. A man could take pride in that.

His hands found a fresh grip of the ax handle. The branches had to be lopped off and shorter sections cut off of the log to be loaded into the wagon.

His ax was raised for the first swing when he heard the shrill yelling of the Sioux. He froze momentarily until his eyes picked them up. He saw flashes of their movement among the trees several hundred yards away. It wasn't an attack. He doubted that more than twenty Indians dashed in and out between the trees.

He heard the guns signal the fort from Pilot Hill, and Fetterman was reacting wrong. He should have pulled his detachment tighter about the wagons and withdrawn his entire command. Instead, he was in full charge at the Sioux. His

97

evaluation of the few numbers was falsely placed on only what he saw.

"Hold it," Portugee yelled. "It's a decoy." That was an old Indian trick, putting out bait to lure an enemy into ambush.

He doubted that Fetterman even heard him above the yelling and the wind. If he had, it wasn't enough to stop him. Portugee raged as he ran toward his wagon. He tossed the ax into it and reached for the step while at a dead run. His foot slipped on a snow-covered tread, and he almost fell. His body slammed into the wagon, and he grabbed for any hold he could find. His muscles strained, then held him, and he pulled himself up. His knee throbbed from impact on the wagon, and he breathed hard. He was glad he had taken the necessary time to turn the wagon around. Other drivers and woodchoppers raced for their wagons. He had the team in a run just as the last woodchopper hurled himself into the bed of Portugee's wagon.

He stood in the box and lashed the animals, and their speed made the wagon careen and lurch. He would look like a damned fool, if he called this ruse wrong, and Fetterman chased off a handful of Sioux.

He looked back at the rattle of gunfire and couldn't see a thing. Fetterman's charge had already carried him into the cover of the trees. Portugee used every obscenity at his command. The goddamned fool, he said over and over.

He climbed that rise, and the fort was in view. Somebody had responded fast to Pilot Hill's signaling. A column of cavalry streamed out of the opened gates, and one of them dragged a caisson behind him. At this distance, Portugee would say it was a six-pounder. He thought several times it would turn over. It bounced high every time its wheels struck a snow-hidden rock.

Portugee pulled out of the beaten track to give the cavalry all the room they wanted, and the other wagons followed him.

He stopped the team just as the rescue detail reached him.

Carrington led the column, and his face was set. Portugee stood and gave him a pointing direction. He caught Carrington's grim nod before he was by.

"You ain't going back there?" somebody in the bed asked in dismay.

"I am not," Portugee snapped. He hadn't gone crazy. He lifted the reins, putting the team into motion again.

He rolled into the fort, and white faces stared up at him. He shook his head. He couldn't tell them a thing. He grabbed his rifle and jumped out. Somebody else could unhitch his team this time.

He climbed up to the walkway, and men lined the wall. Every face was stamped with the strain of agonized waiting. The gates had been slammed shut and barred, and Portugee was in favor of that. Nobody knew what would develop from this. If it was a full attack, the fort was in bad shape. With Carrington's column, almost half of the fort's fighting force was outside the walls.

He couldn't see; he had to depend upon his hearing, and the wind cruelly treated that. It was blowing in the wrong direction, and it played tricks on Portugee. He couldn't be certain he heard gunfire, and he could feel sweat trickling down his body under his clothing. Surely, Carrington hadn't made the mistake of driving deeper after the Sioux.

He heard the blast of the six-pounder, a heavier, deeper report. The wind didn't fool him on that. Carrington had gotten off one shot, and even if it was off target, it would be effective. The Indians dreaded artillery, and without a shell scoring, it could break up a charge.

He looked down, and women were gathered on the ground below him. The women were out, and every face was the same anguished mask. He saw Mrs. Grummond and nodded to her, but she wasn't watching him. Her eyes were fixed on the gates, waiting for them to open again.

This kind of waiting was cruel pressure on a man; it was far worse on a woman.

"Do you see them?" a voice shouted at him. The question

99

was repeated over and over, and Portugee wanted to yell against them. He hadn't seen anything yet, and he would report as he could when he did.

He went limp with relief as Carrington's column came into view. It was in close order; it was a withdrawal, not a retreat. He waited until the last cavalryman came into sight. The caisson was with the cavalry. Carrington hadn't lost any equipment. As far as Portugee could tell not a saddle was empty. He blew out a gusty sigh. Carrington was a damned lucky man to come out of it this well.

He waited until he could recognize individuals. Carrington rode in the lead, and two officers were behind him. Did Carrington take other officers with him? Portugee couldn't remember.

"Open those gates," he roared. "They're coming back."

He hurried down to join Mrs. Grummond, and the strain in her face had aged her twenty years. "George's all right, Mrs. Grummond."

Her eyes closed, and she reeled. He thought she was going to faint, and his hands reached out to steady her.

Her eyes opened with his touch, and tears shone in them. "Thank God." The prayer was barely audible. Her voice strengthened. "I'm all right, Mr. Phillips."

He wanted to lead her away, at least, to someplace where she could sit down, but she wouldn't have it. Her color was better, but she wouldn't be fully assured until she actually saw her husband.

Portugee seethed as he stood beside her and waited. This was no place for a woman, particularly when one had as much on her mind as she did.

Why are you raving at somebody else? he rebuked himself. You've got Hattie here, too.

He watched the troopers ride in a double file into the fort. Carrington hadn't gotten completely off. Two of the men showed bloodstains, and they weren't steady in their saddles. Portugee couldn't see anything that drastically changed his first thought. Carrington was a lucky man.

CHAPTER THIRTEEN

Portugee didn't sit in on the last meeting Carrington held. It seemed as though it lasted forever, and Portugee shifted his weight a dozen times as he waited for that door to open.

Fetterman, Powell, and Grummond finally came out. Portugee couldn't read anything in Powell's face, but Fetterman's eyes were furious. Powell saw Portugee and dropped back to join him. Portugee fell into step with him. He didn't have to ask where they were heading. A man needed whiskey, even Lyford's bad whiskey, to unravel his jangled nerves.

"Did the colonel chew Fetterman?" he asked.

Powell shook his head, and Portugee didn't press the matter further. Powell would talk about it when he wanted to.

They walked into the sutler's, and it wasn't as crowded as usual, but then it was early. Fetterman wasn't here, and Portugee liked that.

They sat down at a table, and Powell ordered whiskey for them. Kathy had something on her mind, but she couldn't quite get it out. She made several false starts, and Portugee curiously watched her. Hutson wasn't here, and Portugee wondered if there had been a quarrel between them.

"Something's bothering her," he observed when she turned away with their order.

"That describes everybody in the fort," Powell grunted.

Portugee could ask about the wounded troopers without prying. "How bad are the two men?"

"They'll make it," Powell answered. That heavy brooding shadowed his eyes. "But they'll be off duty for some time."

Kathy came back and set the drinks on the table. Again, she wanted to say something, and the words wouldn't come out.

Portugee drank half of his glass and waited for its warmth to steal through him. At least, a man wasn't disappointed in that from this whiskey.

Powell smiled sourly at him. "You want to hear about it, don't you?"

Portugee laughed. "I live here too."

That brought back Powell's unhappy smile. "And wish you didn't."

"I could think of other places. The colonel moved in a hurry."

"He did. It pulled Fetterman out of a jam, though I doubt he's ready to admit it."

"The last I saw of him he was chasing the decoy. I yelled." Portugee gave Fetterman the benefit of the doubt. "Maybe he didn't hear me."

Powell's snort said he had some doubts about that too. "Maybe he's beginning to learn. Animal instinct alone to survive should teach a man." Powell shrugged. "Call it what you want. But he didn't ride into the ambush. He was in a strong defense when the colonel found him."

"Could he have held it?"

"He thinks he could. Carrington doesn't. He says two or three hundred Sioux were readying for an attack. They were driving in when an artillery shell changed their minds. Fetterman refuses to believe he was in trouble up to his neck. I don't know what kept Carrington from tearing into him. The colonel had more sense. He was happy to withdraw with only a couple of wounded men."

"Didn't Fetterman comment on that?"

"He wanted to; it was all over his face." Powell grimaced. "He lost another chance to cover himself with glory."

Both men ruminated over that. That desire ran in some

102

men in a strong vein. Portugee was glad that it didn't run in him. He called a good day any one he got through.

He broke the silence. "That meeting took long enough, Captain."

Powell nodded. "We were discussing a better way to get wood."

There wasn't any. No wood had been brought in today, and Portugee visualized the woodpiles, seeing the inroad just a day's use would cut into them.

"And you didn't find one," he said softly.

"No." Powell's negative was a clipped sound.

Portugee regarded him with reflective eyes. The impasse was grinding the captain's soul. Hell, all of them were fearing the effect.

"What's the answer?"

"We're to double the guard," Powell said wearily. "And not go so far after it."

Portugee wanted to protest that. Unless they went deeper into the woods, the better timber was cut. What Powell proposed meant cutting the scrubby stuff. It would take that much longer to fill up the wagons.

Powell's eyes mocked him. "That isn't a satisfactory solution, is it?"

Portugee could have given him a vehement negative, but what good would that do? Carrington was driven by his necessity, and he took the only out he could see. No wonder Fetterman writhed under the colonel's decision. This was more of that passive defense.

Portugee drained his glass. Those days, he wanted one at a time, were going to be harder to get.

"Another drink?" Powell asked.

"Sure." And another one after that and maybe a couple more. Maybe tonight, he would need Hattie's help, but she wouldn't berate him.

His grin angered Powell. "I'm glad you see something funny."

Portugee shook his head. "Not funny at all." He faced

the door and saw Hutson come in. He envied the man. Kathy would erase the pressure on him, for a few hours at least.

"I'll tell you one thing, Captain." He saw Kathy hurry toward Hutson. "I'll never go out again under Fetterman. I don't think he's learned a damned thing."

Powell grunted, and Portugee understood it. Agreement with him would be a form of disloyalty. Even if an officer disliked another, he wouldn't comment unfavorably about him.

He put idle attention on the table where Hutson sat. Kathy stood beside him, and they seemed to be arguing about something. Portugee was sorry for Hutson. Maybe that pressure wasn't going to be lifted.

Whatever they argued about had to do with him and Powell, for he saw them glance several times this way. She was prodding Hutson into something, for Hutson got to his feet. He hesitated by his chair, and there was more talk between them. Neither of them looked too happy. Hutson looked as though he argued about something, and Kathy brushed his words aside.

Evidently, she won out, for Hutson turned and came toward their table. Whatever was on his mind put a heavy drag in his feet. He stopped at Portugee's and Powell's table, and several emotions were in the molding of his face.

"Captain, could I speak to you? It's a personal matter."

"Sit down," Powell invited.

Hutson sat down, and what he had to say must be hard for his mouth opened, and nothing came out.

"You want to talk to Captain Powell alone?" Portugee asked.

Hutson shook his head. "I guess you know about it anyway."

Portugee grinned inwardly. Those must really be hard words to get out.

"Go ahead," Powell said impatiently.

Portugee glanced at Kathy. She had her eyes fixed on Hutson. She approved of whatever Hutson was going to say, and she did everything she could to let him know her encouragement was behind him.

Maybe the word should be pushing, Portugee thought drily.

"I wonder if this is a bad time to bother the colonel?" Hutson muttered.

Portugee had more trouble keeping his grin hidden this time. Hutson thought it was a bad time, or he wouldn't have asked that question.

"Will you get on with it?" Powell snapped.

Hutson's words tumbled out in a breathless burst. "Kathy and I want to be married now. Would the colonel give his permission?"

Powell looked startled, and Portugee imagined he did too. Powell was the first to recover.

"Good God," he said.

"And you don't want to," Portugee decided. "That was what you were arguing about."

"No, sir." Hutson's denial was vigorous. "I knew what I wanted the first time I saw her. Should I try to see the colonel?"

"With all he's got on his mind," Powell exploded. "You'd be lucky if he didn't throw you out of his office."

"That's what I thought, sir," Hutson said miserably. He turned and dragged back to tell Kathy.

"The young fool, wanting to marry her at this time," Powell said.

Portugee didn't agree with Powell. "Only young, Captain. They feel as though they have to rush things. They don't know how much time they've got left."

"Hell," Powell said, but it wasn't an argument.

They sat silently for several minutes, each man occupied with his thoughts. Portugee felt sorry for Kathy and Hutson. They were not much more than kids. They were pinned in the same box that held everybody. He didn't blame them for grabbing at whatever they could.

Fetterman came in fifteen minutes later. He had been doing

some earlier drinking, but it hadn't relaxed him; it only seemed to feed an inner anger.

He sat down with Grummond, and Portugee wished he could break up that bond. He had an odd hunch that anybody closely associated with Fetterman was going to get hurt. He debated upon talking it over with Mrs. Grummond. It wouldn't do. Even if she agreed with him, her loyalty to her husband would prevent her from saying so.

Fetterman's voice rose above a lull in the talk. "I didn't need help. I was set for those redskinned bastards."

Portugee glanced at Powell and couldn't resist a human impulse. "I told you he hadn't learned a damned thing."

CHAPTER FOURTEEN

Portugee lay beside Hattie, his arm pillowing her head. He had told her about Hutson's predicament and finished by saying, "Hattie, he looked like a whipped dog. That boy really wants to marry her."

"I should hope so," she said indignantly.

He chuckled at her typically feminine remark. "Well, he's going to have to learn to wait a little while."

This was the best hour of the twenty-four, the time before a man slipped into sleep. All the work was done, and the kids were asleep. He could lay here and build up an illusion of security for his family.

Hattie sighed. "That's so hard for the young, John. Don't you suppose Captain Powell would talk to the colonel?"

Portugee remembered Powell's outbreak when he had heard what Hutson had in mind. "He won't. And I don't blame him. Not with everything else Carrington has on his mind."

"When do you think he would?" she asked with a woman's persistence.

"When the Sioux siege is lifted." That would stop her.

It didn't, for she said, "It seems such a pity. This is a rare and beautiful time in a person's life. And because of something they can't help, they can't have it."

He heard her voice but not the words. He was listening to the keening of the wind. It had strengthened in just the last few minutes. It could signify more snow and probably the onslaught of another blizzard. Oh damn it, he groaned.

"Don't you think so?" She nudged him with an elbow. "John, you didn't hear anything I said."

"I did," he protested.

It satisfied her for she didn't pin him down to repeating what she said. "I just hope it works out all right for them."

"I hope that for everybody," he grunted. His eyelids were drooping. "Go to sleep, Hattie." This subject could keep a woman talking for hours.

It was a blizzard when Portugee awakened in the morning. The wind tore at men and animals, and a man dreaded to step out from shelter. But it could work to their advantage. Even the weather-hardened Sioux wouldn't venture out in this unless they were forced.

He stopped in at Wheatley's quarters, and Wheatley and Fisher were dressed. He hadn't been there thirty seconds when another coughing spell hit Wheatley. By the redness of Fisher's nose he had been blowing it steadily.

"You're not going out today," he said.

Mrs. Wheatley was at the stove. She had spent little time on fixing her hair this morning, and locks were down in her face. Her child was crying, and that added to the harassment in her face. She brushed back the hair and raised her voice to her husband.

"You are not going to go out until it gets warmer." She chunked another piece of wood into the stove. It was beginning to get that cherry-red glow, but its heat wasn't enough yet to chase the cold out of the corners.

"Listen to Portugee," she said with resentment. "I can't do anything with him. I didn't get a wink of sleep all night because of his coughing."

Portugee knew a wry amusement. This was a typical morning for a woman and mother. "He isn't going out," he assured her.

He saw he wasn't going to get any more argument out of Wheatley. Wheatley had proved his maleness, and he was glad to give in.

She smiled her thankfulness to Portugee. "Have some breakfast?"

"Ate," he answered. "I just stopped in to see how they're getting along." He walked to the door, opened and shut it quickly behind him to cut down the savage rip of the wind that tried to tear it out of his hands.

He walked to the stables, and he didn't know yet what he would be doing. He had made a promise to himself and Powell that he would never again serve under Fetterman. What he did would depend upon what Fetterman was assigned.

Powell and Hutson were already here, waiting for the last of the detail to report. Portugee thought sourly, this morning will see a lot of malingerers.

Hutson looked miserable, and it wasn't solely the weather causing it. Last night's talk with Powell was causing most of it. At his age a setback seemed so damnably permanent. It usually took ages for a man to learn patience.

"You taking it out?" Portugee asked Powell. At Powell's nod he said, "Then I guess I'll haul wood."

Powell's voice was muffled by the coat collar he had up over his mouth. "It's going to be a hell of a day."

Portugee snorted. "Ain't it already?" Nobody would slack their work today, even though they looked bear-like and awkward in the clothes they had put on. They would work like hell to keep some life in their numbing hands and feet.

He picked up the reins. Woodpiles had to be replenished. "Let's go."

It was the beginning of a succession of dreary days, the severity occasionally lessening, and it was only favorable by comparison. Portugee switched from hauling wood to hauling water, depending on the greater need and also depending on who was in charge. The days rolled by in dull routine, and he hadn't seen a feather. He would give anything to know what Red Cloud was thinking. A man could lull himself into false hope that Red Cloud had given up; at least, for this winter. But he would really be a damned fool to believe that. The fires still burned in the hills around them; the Sioux were still there.

There had been no attacks since Fetterman's brush with the Sioux, and men fretted under the inactivity. He had heard many an argument of what it meant. Too many men said that winter's blows had broken the back of a possible Sioux attack. Portugee kept his mouth shut. Fear put out those foolish arguments. He could point that out, but it would be a form of cruelty to kick away the crutch men so needed. But Portugee thought about it, long and hard. The only thing he could come up with about the inactivity was that the Sioux were shaping a massive attack.

He was chopping ice, cursing its thickness when the realization of the date struck him. My God, this was the twenty-first of December, and he hadn't given a thought to presents for Hattie and the kids. Lyford's place was a poor one to look for presents. They would have to be the usual, ordinary things that life demanded.

He struck another savage blow, and a thin spray of shaved ice sprayed him. Cutting ice was far harder than chopping wood, and the small progress for the cost in effort galled a man.

What a day! Ten inches of snow were on the ground, and the temperature was around zero. He hoped it would moderate before Christmas. He lifted his ax for another stroke and went rigid. Was that a gun report from Pilot Hill? He heard it again, confirmation of what he feared. The wood train was under attack.

"Let's go," he yelled at the men with him. He ran to the wagon and tossed his ax into the bed. The water wagon wasn't under attack and probably wouldn't be, but Portugee had to find out what was going on.

At the water gate he had to scream his demands for somebody to open it. He glared at the man who had been so slow in unbarring it.

He drove the wagon to the stables and turned it over to a corporal.

"Where's the wood train?" he demanded.

The corporal's eyes were harried. "They were going to cut along Big Piney, Portugee."

That would be along the road south of the creek. It was about a mile and a half from the fort, and Portugee's mouth went tight as he heard the rattle of gunfire coming from the area.

Somebody yelled from the wall, and Portugee scurried up a ladder. The Sioux were getting reckless. Maybe two dozen of them were on the Bozeman Trail where it crossed Big Piney north of the fort. They were close enough for the wind to carry their voices to him.

"You sons-of-bitches," one of the voices yelled.

Portugee didn't get the rest of it, but it would be only a further taunting. The oath didn't surprise him. Oaths were about the first English an Indian learned.

Carrington was on the howitzer, and he shelled them. The burst flushed more of them out of the brush, and all of them fled. It was too bad the shell was short of the target.

Portugee didn't think any real threat was in the Sioux he had seen. It was only a diversion to keep attention off of the attack on the train.

Carrington did too, for he scrambled down the ladder, bawling for Powell. The two men met on the parade grounds, and Portugee was close enough behind Carrington to hear him say, "Captain Powell, take a force and relieve the wood-cutters. Drive those Indians over the creek, but don't go any farther."

Powell nodded, but before he could turn away Fetterman came up.

"If anyone goes except the colonel," he said, "I want to be that officer."

Carrington gnawed on his lip, and Portugee knew what disturbed him. He wanted to refuse Fetterman, but Fetterman ranked Powell.

"Granted, Captain." The gray weariness seemed to have increased in Carrington's face.

That goddamned fetish of seniority, Portugee raved. Whenever it could be homage was paid to it. Portugee wanted to yell, you're making a mistake.

Powell's set, black expression showed that he was seething too, over this replacement.

"Take infantry and cavalrymen with you," Carrington said. "You are to go to the relief of the train and no farther. Under no circumstances are you to go beyond Lodge Trail Ridge."

"Understood, sir."

Portugee wished he knew what that shine in Fetterman's eyes meant. If he did know, he couldn't do anything about it. Carrington was the only man here who could.

"Pick your officers, Captain."

Hutson stood a hundred yards from them, and Fetterman threw a malicious look at him. It said Hutson wouldn't be one of his officers. "Mr. Grummond to lead the cavalry, sir."

Portugee groaned as he thought of Mrs. Grummond. Grummond would be eager to take it. The damned fool didn't think of Mrs. Grummond or anything else except winning Fetterman's approval.

Fetterman saluted Carrington and wheeled, yelling his orders as he ran.

Sergeants picked up those orders and gave them more volume. Men poured out of barracks, some of them cutting off and heading for the stables, the rest of them forming on the parade grounds.

They were muffled up to their eyes, and that looked like misery in them. Right now, Portugee suspected that only the weather was on their minds. He prayed that nothing else would supplant it.

Wheatley and Fisher came up, and they carried their Henrys. He knew what they intended doing.

His face was wrathful as he demanded, "Where in the hell do you think you're going?"

"Aw, Portugee." Wheatley wouldn't meet his eyes. "Those damned walls were driving me crazy."

Portugee didn't doubt that. Wheatley was an active man, and confining him with walls was as bad as caging a wild animal.

Fisher grinned. "He's talking for me."

Portugee swore at that grin. Fisher never took anything with the proper seriousness.

Wheatley lifted his Henry. "I thought we could give them a taste of these. It'll put a little more respect in them."

"Come with us, Portugee," Fisher wheedled.

"No," Portugee said coldly. He had his reason, and he put it into words. "Fetterman's leading it out."

Wheatley's eyebrows rose, but he showed no other reaction. If Fisher felt objection to Portugee's reason, he didn't express it.

"You know how I feel about him. I'm not going to let some fool thought in his head risk my hide." He had Hattie and the kids to think about. Wheatley had a couple of good reasons, himself.

"Aw, Portugee," Wheatley said and stopped.

Portugee's answer was in his silence. Maybe all three of them had the same streak of stubbornness. Wheatley and Fisher had made up their minds, and nothing was going to change them.

"Suit yourselves." Portugee stepped back. He had said all he could.

Wheatley and Fisher hurried toward the stables, almost as though they wanted to run to get away from him. Portugee knew a pang of misery. This was the first breach to show between them.

He joined Powell and watched Fetterman's infantrymen assemble. In reality, they gathered with speed, but this was the cruel time. It stretched minutes until they seemed like hours.

Fetterman mounted and moved his foot soldiers toward

the gates. The infantry was ready to move sooner than the cavalry.

Hutson's eyes were bitter. "Damn him. He tries to grab everything. And he doesn't care who he steps on."

Portugee pierced him with a look. Hutson must have expected to accompany Powell. From his words and expression he felt the replacement as keenly as Powell did.

Portugee counted the infantry as its ranks passed him. Carrington was sending out forty-seven men. It was a strong force but not a very mobile one.

He turned his head at the sound of horsemen. Grummond was bringing up his cavalry. Portugee imagined that neither man nor animal wanted to leave the fort. He amended the thought when he looked at Grummond. It didn't apply to him. Grummond's face held a blazing eagerness.

Carrington left the parade grounds and climbed to the sentry platform at the gate. Portugee and Powell followed him.

Grummond's troops trotted toward the gates.

Carrington stopped them there. "Mr. Grummond, did Captain Fetterman give you my orders?"

"Yes, sir." Grummond repeated them. "We are not to go beyond Lodge Trail Ridge."

"Do you understand them?"

"Yes, sir."

Carrington returned Grummond's salute. "Good luck, Mr. Grummond."

Portugee counted the cavalry as it passed through the gates. Wheatley and Fisher rode with them, and neither of them looked at him.

A sudden thought gagged Portugee. Grummond had twenty-seven men. Counting the two officers and Wheatley and Fisher, it added up to a total of eighty. Fetterman's brag came vividly back to him. Fetterman had what he wanted; enough men to cut a swath through the Sioux nation.

He climbed after Powell to the walkway, and it was lined

with anxious men. This was the moment that made them all alike. Tension had them in its cruel grip.

It was snowing hard, and under its blanket he wouldn't be able to see those men too far. He found himself breathing with more effort. Physical effort wasn't the only thing that could burden a man's breathing.

He watched Fetterman's infantry diminish in size. Grummond would catch up with the main body before long.

Fetterman met light opposition as he occupied the ridge in good skirmish order. Portugee heard the reports of rifles. If he couldn't see those rifles, he could imagine the flashes of muzzle fire and the pocking of the snow under the impact of bullets.

That small body of Sioux had no intention of establishing full contact for they were fleeing. He saw small figures of pony and rider drop over the ridge and disappear. They were running before Fetterman.

He turned his head at another signal from Pilot Hill. The Indians, attacking the wood train, must be withdrawing too. All Fetterman had to do was to join up with it, then pull back to the fort. Portugee wasn't the only man, on the walk, who sighed.

His mouth sagged. Fetterman didn't look as though he had that intention at all. He was swinging away from the direction of the train.

He looked at Hutson, remembering Hutson's remark about Fetterman knocking him out of his opportunity.

"Maybe you'll find out just how lucky you are."

CHAPTER FIFTEEN

Fisher drew a bead on an Indian an instant before his pony dropped out of sight over the ridge. He grunted with pleasure as the Indian fell, bouncing and rolling before the body came to a stop.

"Got mine," he said.

Wheatley shook his head in disgust. "Missed mine. It's this damned snow."

Fisher chuckled. A man had to have some excuse for his bad shooting. The Indians were in flight. This should about wrap it up.

Alarm touched Wheatley's face. "What's Fetterman doing?"

Worry creased Fisher's forehead. Fetterman wasn't taking the wood road south of the Piney toward the wagon train. Instead, he waved the infantry north, and that meant he intended to cross the creek.

"This is the first time we ever went against one of Portugee's feelings," Fisher muttered.

Wheatley's awareness of that was in his face. He looked over his shoulder, and the fort was still within view. "We can turn back," he snapped. He was deeply troubled. The sharpness of his tone said that.

Fisher shook his head. Neither of them wanted that. He could visualize the scornful appraisal on men's faces. Everyone of them would know they had tucked their tails between their legs; Portugee particularly.

"No," he said. His face brightened. He thought he knew

what Fetterman had in mind. "He's trying to outflank the Indians who attacked the train."

"Maybe," Wheatley said flatly.

The word carried no agreement, and Fisher's worry returned. Had they bought into a pot they didn't know anything about? Damnit! He missed Portugee.

Grummond and his cavalry caught up with the infantry before Fetterman crossed the creek bed. The snow hid the spots where the ice was thin, and men cursed as they broke through and wet their boots. They increased the speed and length of their stride, hoping to be across before the water had time to soak through leather.

Fetterman headed northwest up the Piney. The cavalry was on his right flank as skirmishers along the east side.

Fisher kept twisting in the saddle to keep an eye on the infantry. Wasn't Grummond aware of how much the distance between the two forces was growing? The ridge which Fetterman was using was in two sections, the north one smaller and lower. Grummond was about a mile ahead, and the ridge was making its final descent to Peno Creek. Nothing was in his head but to catch the Indians ahead of him.

None of it looked good to Fisher. He couldn't see anything in the valley ahead, but that didn't mean Indians weren't around. There had to be something more to make his skin prickle like this.

"Jim," he said. "We're getting in too deep." He hadn't more than gotten the words out when it felt as though he had been clubbed in the stomach. His eyes bulged over a sagging mouth.

Indians jumped up from every view. Sioux had been lying in the grass on both slopes. Mounted Cheyenne appeared from the west, and dismounted Sioux came out of the little flatland to the east. Now, mounted Sioux galloped into sight from behind the rocks that had hidden them.

"Holy Jesus," Fisher said in awe. "There must be a million of them."

"Close enough," Wheatley said and looked about for a

place to make a stand. He and Fisher had the sixteen-shot Henrys, and the cavalrymen were armed with the seven-shot Spencers. They could throw out enough firepower to make even the maddened horde of Indians hesitate.

But Grummond didn't intend to make a stand. He wheeled his horse, and he was yelling. His words couldn't be heard above the deluge of war cries. He gestured madly and finally made himself understood. They were pulling back to join Fetterman.

Fisher and Wheatley looked at each other, and the same thought was in their eyes. Retreating was sure death. The running cavalry would be hit on both flanks and from the front and rear. Grummond couldn't possibly make it. Anything else was the slimmest of chances, but the combined firepower of the Henrys and Spencers might hold off the Indians. Grummond was throwing away the last chance.

They didn't need words to communicate. They swung off their horses and ran for the clump of boulders, a dozen yards ahead. Those horses were gone, and Fisher knew the stab of regret. He wiped out the regret; he didn't have time to think of anything else but Indians.

They crouched panting behind the boulder, rifle butts to shoulders and waited. Now the sorrowful thoughts came back. A man could think of so many things in the last, few seconds allotted him.

The Indians poured in from every side, and the Henrys kept talking. Fisher and Wheatley were seasoned frontiersmen, and they didn't panic. Neither of them wasted a shot. A trigger was only pulled whenever the muzzle was on a target, and the rifles cost the Sioux a frightful toll.

The empty shells piled up on the snow, and they stopped shooting only when they had to reload.

For a fleeting moment of hope, Fisher thought they might check them, for an Indian couldn't face these kinds of losses. But the horde was too great, and the waves behind the first one pushed it ahead. The smell of victory was in those frenzied faces, and they couldn't be turned.

They poured over Wheatley and Fisher as they were reloading. Fisher's fingers worked in desperate haste, and the red wave poured in over the boulders while another wave rolled in right behind them.

Wheatley's hoarse cry jerked Fisher's head toward him. Wheatley was standing and trying to retain his feet. But his legs were buckling as he tried to pull an arrow from his throat. He toppled all at once, and before he hit the ground, a half-dozen more arrows pierced him.

Fisher's cry was yanked out of him by loss and despair. A brave's crazed yelling was right in his ear. He didn't have time enough to look around and see how close the Indian was before a lance ran him through. Oh God, Portugee, you were right. The merciful blackness wiped his mind clean.

Grummond led the cavalry's frantic retreat. All around them the savages were closing in. A running man can put up no defense, and to the Indians, this was no more difficult than bringing down a buffalo in a hunt. They raced along on either side of the cavalry, and some of them were only a dozen yards away. A rain of arrows whistled in, and out of that multitude some of them had to find targets. A cavalryman groaned and slid out of his saddle, and before a dozen strides were gained another one fell. The horrible attrition cut them down, and half of the cavalry was wiped out before they reached Fetterman.

Hope rose in Grummond that he might make it. He wasn't two hundred yards from where the infantry was when an arrow buried deep into his side. His hands fell away from the reins, and the horse had no guide. Grummond straightened until he stood in the stirrups. Other arrows found their mark, and Grummond pitched out of the saddle.

A dozen cavalrymen reached Fetterman's rocks, and the Indians followed them all the way in. The infantry threw up a wall of fire, and the Indians broke against it. Less than half of the original cavalrymen jumped from their horses and dashed the remaining few yards to the rocks. Two

Indians, who had followed them all the way, slid from their ponies and slammed against the rocks.

The others broke and streamed by on both sides of Fetterman. One of his men screamed in a torment of agony. Two others fell under the hail of arrows. The rifle fire followed them until it was useless to shoot further.

Fetterman screamed at them to conserve ammunition. Even as cold as it was, his face ran sweat, and he mopped it with a shaky hand. He regretted so many things; the loss of the cavalry as a striking force, the loss of the seven-shot Spencers they carried. Two of the cavalrymen had lost their rifles, and he put a bitter curse against them. He did not berate himself. He was only trying to do what he had been sent out here for. My God, how did he know that such unbelievable numbers were in hiding, waiting for him?

He checked their position and could see nothing he could do to improve it. The infantry was arrayed in a circle, trying to shelter themselves as best as they could in the rocks.

He cursed the single-shot Springfields, the infantry had been issued. What he would do for a Spencer in every man's hands. Even those old Springfields had cost the Indians, for bodies lay around the rocks. For an instant, he hoped that first breaking of the Indians meant they had their bellies full, but they were reforming again.

They raced back, and it was inconceivable that bows and arrows would come again against gunfire. He recalled a tactic that had been so effective in the Civil War.

"Fire in alternate ranks," he yelled. One rank would shoot while the other reloaded. There would be no lapse in the wall of lead the Indians met. "Hold your fire until I give the order."

The blanket of snow was blackening under the oncoming numbers, and the sheer mass of them was mind-stultifying. It was more than enough to panic an old campaigner, and the recruits were shoved into blind terror. They wasted ammunition at long range, and most of the shots weren't aimed. For a short time, the ranks fired alternately, and then the order was forgotten. Men pulled triggers as fast as they could without really seeing what they were trying to hit.

Fetterman heard men scream for more cartridges, and it stunned him. It wasn't possible that those men could be out. Did it mean that all of the ammunition was getting low? He had brought twenty-eight hundred rounds with him, and with that amount of ammunition, they should be blasting great holes in the oncoming horde. But if all of those shots had any effect on the front ranks of the Indians, he couldn't see it. He raved at his men to aim, to hold their shots until they were sure. If a man heard him he couldn't see it, for that wild, frantic shooting keep on unabated.

The arrows flew in from all degrees of the compass, and Fetterman couldn't believe his force was melting so rapidly. Some men fell silently, while others died in screaming agony. An icy despair gripped his heart. Nothing could stop the Sioux this time.

Perhaps a dozen men were still on their feet when the Indians rode over them. But that was nothing but a small hummock of sand, trying to stem an onrushing flood. For a tick of time, white strained faces stared into distorted red ones, then the war clubs smashed them down.

Fetterman was the last to crumple. His pistol was empty, and an arrow was in his shoulder. He was helpless, but he tried to leap at one of them and drag him from his pony. The war club shattered his last conscious thought.

The hideous din should have stopped. There should have been a silence, a moment of grieving for the dead. But the Indians didn't recognize that silence. They were drunk with their winning, and the hacking and slashing started. Knives rose and fell, drawing their reddening tracery. More arrows were released into lifeless bodies, turning bodies into macabre pincushions. Some of the Indians picked up the soldiers' guns and pumped shots into the unresisting flesh. The celebration seemed to be endless.

CHAPTER SIXTEEN

Portugee and Powell were with Carrington on the lookout post from a roof. It was snowing much harder, and the wind drove it into fantastic patterns. The wind had increased in just the last half-hour, and it cut like a knife.

Carrington scanned the scene through his glasses and muttered, "He must be trying to outflank the Indians who attacked the train."

The words carried no conviction. Portugee was rigid with anxiety. Turn back, he prayed. Turn back.

He couldn't see the sun because of the lowering gray clouds, but he judged it to be around noon when he heard the first irregular outbursts of firing. The sound was thin and reedy, and he judged the distance had to be three miles or more from the fort. The firing had to be Fetterman's for most of the Indians carried bow and arrows and lances.

"He has caught up with him," Carrington said. He couldn't put encouragement into it. The sickness in his face belied his words.

Not when the firing comes from that far away, Portugee thought. Fetterman disobeyed orders; he had gone farther than he should. Carrington's face said he knew it too.

A horseman, preceding an ambulance, galloped back into the fort, and the ambulance team was under heavy whipping. This was more bad news. The assistant post surgeon and ambulance had been sent out to join Fetterman's command.

Major Dubois galloped all the way across the parade grounds and jerked his horse to a halt. He looked up at

Carrington and reported, "Captain Fetterman has gone beyond the ridge, sir."

Carrington accepted the information with a brief closing of his eyes. He was a man with iron control not to let any more emotion show.

The firing started again with much more volume this time. Carrington listened to it and said, "Fetterman has ordered firing by file."

Portugee heard the regular crashing of the volleys. Let Carrington take what hope he could from the sound. Portugee couldn't find any. It only meant that Fetterman was under heavy attack. The regular crashing of the file volleys faded, dropping off into sporadic shots. That slowly died out, and Portugee ached as he strained to hear more. He heard a few more scattered shots, then the blanket of silence was smothering him.

"Guard," Carrington yelled.

The guard raced over to him, and Carrington snapped, "Call out every man. Open the magazine and issue guns and ammunition. I want wagons and ambulances hitched up. Inform Captain Ten Eyck he will command the detachment that will find and strengthen Captain Fetterman."

The guard saluted, whipped around, and was off again at a dead run. He tried to bawl orders as he ran, and his exertion made his words jerky.

Portugee heard Carrington with only half of his attention. Did he hear a few more shots?

Carrington made a ghastly attempt at a smile. "I think that Captain Fetterman has killed or repulsed them. If so, I am afraid that the Sioux will gather again for another rush."

Portugee's eyes seared him. Carrington couldn't even lie to himself. "I'm going with Ten Eyck." He didn't have to explain. Carrington knew Wheatley and Fisher were out there.

Carrington's nod was deathly weary. "Yes, Mr. Phillips."

The parade ground was a madhouse. Sergeants barked orders and men and horses raced into position. Portugee saddled his horse and was in time to join Ten Eyck. Some of those men had just rushed out of barracks, and their shoulders were whitening.

Ten Eyck led thirty cavalrymen through the gates. Portugee looked back, and men were climbing into the wagons. Most of them were civilians. Dear God, Portugee thought. Are we down to this, calling out the civilians?

Ten Eyck put the column into double-quick time. The horses didn't want to face that wind, and they kept trying to turn their heads against it. A man was kept busy, sawing on the reins to get some obedience into his horse.

Ten Eyck led the way across Big Piney Creek and turned up the Bozeman Trail. The Trail ran through the gap that lead to the big ridge. Portugee's head jerked to rigid attention. Was that screams and groans he heard?

It wasn't repeated, but he couldn't relax. Ten Eyck halted at the top of the main ridge. Portugee knew why he stopped. Every man strained to see or hear some indication that Fetterman was still alive.

Portugee saw activity down there, but none of it was made by blue uniforms. Maybe a hundred Indians milled around that point of rocks. They saw Ten Eyck for they waved their bows and taunted him to come down and fight.

Don't let them suck you down there, Portugee prayed. Not until you can see that you can do some good. If Ten Eyck had such an impulse, all he had to do was to raise his eyes above the Indians around the rocks. Hundreds of them were on the ridge beyond the valley. More were down in the valley and on the opposite buttes. The heat of battle was still in many of them. They looked as if they were crazy as they dashed up and down the slopes.

Ten Eyck beckoned Portugee to him. "What's your estimate, Mr. Phillips?"

Portugee grunted. So Ten Eyck had seen them. "Two thousand. Maybe more. I never saw so goddamned many Indians gathered in one place before."

Portugee's number didn't change Ten Eyck's face. The paling was there before he asked.

He nodded as though Portugee only confirmed his estimation and called a messenger to him.

"Tell the colonel to send everything he can," he said to the man. "Men and artillery. Report to him there may be two thousand Indians out here." He hesitated over his next words. "Inform him that I am afraid Captain Fetterman's command is gone. For God's sake, Corporal, make the fastest trip you ever made."

"Yes, sir." The corporal wheeled his horse and kicked it into a dead run.

That same fear, that Ten Eyck expressed, was an icy sheath around Portugee's heart. The ice melted a little. Wheatley and Fisher had been in tough scrapes before. Maybe they had slipped through the tightening noose. Hard, cold logic extinguished the tiny flame of hope. Not even Jim and Isaac could make it through this many Indians.

Portugee advised pulling back right now, but Ten Eyck refused to do that.

"I can't leave right now, Portugee. I have to wait for the return of the courier. And I have to be able to tell Colonel Carrington exactly what happened."

Portugee nodded. He understood Ten Eyck's position, but he wasn't in agreement with it.

He steeled himself to wait out the leaden minutes. He knew he wasn't giving the rider enough time, but damnit, how long did it take a rider to make the round trip to the fort?

He was talking to Ten Eyck when the messenger returned. His eyes widened; the rider was on Gray Eagle, Carrington's thoroughbred. Carrington was well aware of the urgency, or he would never have loaned that horse.

"I passed the wagons and ambulances on the way back, sir," the messenger reported. "Colonel Carrington is sending everybody he can. They'll be here soon."

Carrington had written a message, and the man passed it to Ten Eyck.

Ten Eyck's eyes dropped to the paper, and the courier said, "He wants your opinion of the number of Indians."

Ten Eyck's eyes scanned the valley. "Not as many as there was. But still too damned many," he said grimly. "Tell him the situation hasn't eased."

"Yes, sir," the man said and whirled Gray Eagle.

Ten Eyck's eyes went back to Carrington's message, and his face blackened as he read it. "I want you to see this." He handed it to Portugee, and his lips were a compressed line.

You must unite with Fetterman, Carrington wrote. *You could have saved two miles toward the scene of action, if you had taken Lodge Trail Ridge.*

"Why goddamn it," Portugee exploded. "Does he realize if we took Lodge Trail, we'd still be floundering through the ravines and snowbanks."

Ten Eyck's eyes smoldered, but he tried to make an excuse for rank. "The colonel doesn't realize that Fetterman took Bozeman Trail." His anger slipped its moorings. "He will when he finds out we only followed Fetterman."

Portugee's wrath couldn't be appeased. "Doesn't he believe that Fetterman and the others are gone?"

"He hopes not," Ten Eyck said flatly.

The approach of the wagons and ambulances choked off the remainder of Portugee's hot words. He doubted that the artillery had been put into the wagons before they left. The messenger hadn't been able to reach the fort before the wagons rolled. Very few soldiers were in the wagons, but forty civilians climbed out of them.

Turning to look down into the valley he stared in disbelief as the Indians were beginning to leave. Certainly, it wasn't Ten Eyck's meager force that prompted them to withdraw. Maybe it was because they thought the wagons carried artillery, the awful guns that spoke often in a loud voice.

Bridger came up to him, and Portugee turned at his touch.

"It looks like we're in a mess, Portugee."

"Worse than that, Jim. It's a massacre."

Bridger whistled.

Ten Eyck was moving his cavalry, and Bridger asked, "What's he doing?"

Portugee pointed at the wave of Indians disappearing over a skyline. "Maybe that's his reason."

Ten Eyck could go in closer now. He had to bring back a factual report of what had happened to Fetterman.

Ten Eyck moved down the main ridge to the smaller one and stopped men and wagons there.

"I'd like to go have a look," Portugee said.

Bridger squinted at that empty skyline, then nodded a grudging agreement.

Portugee told Ten Eyck where they were going, and Ten Eyck sighed. "I can't order you to go, but I would like to know exactly what happened down there."

"We figured it that way," Portugee said gruffly. He had to know what had happened to Fisher and Wheatley.

He swung off his horse, and Bridger joined him on the ground. The wind had a sweep at the trail here, and the drifting wasn't as bad. But just off of the Trail the drifts started. They would wear out a horse in a hurry. They breasted some of the drifts, leaving them panting, and avoided what others they could. The wind wasn't as fierce here, but the white curtain fell steadily. Their heads turned constantly as they tried to cover all points of the compass at once. Nothing moved against the mantle of snow.

They saw the bodies scattered about the point of rocks before they reached it. Their walk slowed, and a horror grew in their eyes. The snow blanket was beginning to cover everything, but it couldn't hide it all. No past experience could prepare them for the impact of what they saw. All around them sightless eyes stared at the sky, and around each body, a pool of blood had crimsoned the snow.

Minds had to be forced to accept the degree of the muti-

128

lation. Portugee blew out a hard breath, and Bridger muttered, "They went crazy, didn't they?"

Portugee nodded. Indians did that after a winning.

The bodies were stripped, and it was hard to identify some of the agony-torn faces. But Wheatley and Fisher weren't here.

Bridger stood over Fetterman's body, and Portugee moved over to him. Fetterman, like all the rest, had died hard.

"He was a damned fool," Bridger said.

It was true, but the past was all wiped out, and Portugee wanted something more forgiving. "He was a brave man." Fetterman had all of these dead on his soul. He had enough to face without Portugee further blaming him.

He pointed ahead of him. Another body lay some two hundred yards away, and a line of bodies stretched out beyond that one.

Portugee stopped beside the body of George Grummond. Oh Jesus, he mourned. Who is going to tell her?

He looked at another body, some fifteen yards away. "Grummond's cavalry. They didn't make it back to join Fetterman."

They followed the grisly trail. Two more lay at the out-thrust of rocks. Portugee didn't have to get any closer to know who they were.

Wheatley and Fisher were stripped like all the others, and their bodies knew the same mutilation as the others. Portugee stood over them a long moment, and the smarting in his eyes increased.

Bridger respected that silence, then finally said, "They put up one hell of a fight."

The spent cartridges around Wheatley and Fisher were mute testimony to that.

"Yes," Portugee said. The simple word was the finest accolade he could give them. They had tried to check the rush of the Sioux to give the cavalry enough time to retreat. The fact that they hadn't been able to do it was no faulting of them. Nobody could have.

Bridger looked uneasily about him. "It's time to be going, Portugee."

"Not until we take them with us," Portugee said. He didn't blame Bridger for being concerned about the Sioux returning. The same concern lay uneasily in the back of Portugee's head, but he didn't think the Sioux would return right away. They had celebrating to do. The sick gorge rose in his throat as he thought of all those bucks wearing parts of uniforms. He jerked his thoughts from that. But Bridger was right. There was no sense wasting any more time here than was necessary.

He walked to where Ten Eyck had a clear view of him and waved for him to come down. "The ambulances," he yelled and thought Ten Eyck understood.

The drivers drove the ambulances down the treacherous slope. Portugee recognized that look on their faces as they looked at the massacre. Some of them were going to be sick.

They loaded the cold-stiffened bodies into the ambulances with all possible haste. Wheatley and Fisher were lifted into the last ambulance, and Portugee knew he would not look at them again. Helpless thoughts churned in his head. Mrs. Wheatley had to be told. This couldn't possibly be kept from her, but there had to be some way to make it as easy as possible for her.

Jim died quick and easy. The words slipped into his mind. He hoped it would do.

They climbed back to the road, and no man breathed freely until they reached it. Portugee hadn't counted the bodies. He didn't have to; he knew how many went out.

The snow didn't look as though it would ever let up, and the wind had a new, savage bite. Portugee shivered, and the cold wasn't the sole cause of it.

CHAPTER SEVENTEEN

Snowbanks were beginning to pile up against the stockade walls as the sad procession passed through the gates. Carrington stood apart from a group of people, all of them waiting for the same news that would lift the fear from them. A woman suddenly screamed. The cavalcade hadn't yet reached her. She couldn't have seen the bodies in the ambulances. Perhaps instinct told her, or she could read it in the grim faces of the living.

Ten Eyck dismounted before Carrington and waved the cavalry and wagons on. He made a gesture, stopping Portugee, and Portugee thought savagely, I can't tell Carrington any more than he can. But he dismounted beside Ten Eyck.

Carrington stood very straight as he received Ten Eyck's report, but he gave the impression of reeling under it.

He's suddenly an old man, Portugee thought; an old man so brittle that one more blow will make him fly apart.

"You are certain, Captain?"

"Portugee went down there and found them. He saw no living survivor."

Portugee sighed. He knew what Carrington begged for. He couldn't tell him anything that would relieve the gray anxiety in his face.

"You surveyed the entire battle site, Mr. Phillips?"

Portugee had to destroy the last hope in the man. "The bodies tally," he said as gently as he could. How could a man still stand and look as though he has stopped breathing. "They put up one hell of a fight, Colonel." He didn't know how good it had been. In Wheatley's and Fisher's case, the empty shells meant something. A trained eye and head, that wouldn't panic, had aimed those bullets. But the empty shells around the soldiers didn't tell him anything. He had no knowledge of those men.

Carrington grasped at the last straw left him. "They cost the Sioux? You saw their dead?"

Portugee had to take even that from him. "The Sioux wouldn't leave their dead and wounded behind them." He found the only solace he could give Carrington. "They were up against a lot of them."

Carrington made an effort to face the hard, cold facts, but he wasn't talking to either of them. "It means that over half of the garrison is wiped out. One hundred and nineteen left, counting the civilians."

It was a sickening summary. Portugee knew that number included the sick and wounded. Ammunition should be low, maybe less than a full box per man.

"Since September, I have begged for men, arms, and ammunition," Carrington muttered.

Ten Eyck and Portugee exchanged worried looks. Was the colonel shattering under this massive blow? The snowfall was increasing, and the howling wind drove it in blinding sheets until a man couldn't see farther than a few yards ahead of him. It could be the beginning of a mountain blizzard, and Portugee knew what they could be. Carrington was literally hemmed in. He couldn't take a step out of the fort. In fact, Portugee couldn't see how he could hold it. One more determined assault by the Sioux, and they would breach the walls.

"Colonel, we've got to do something."

Carrington gave him a dazed look, then from somewhere he found a remaining shred of toughness. He drew what he could out of the brutal facts and made the most he could out of them.

When he faced Ten Eyck, some of the old crisp decision was in his voice. "Captain, release the prisoners from the guardhouse. See that every man is armed and divide the ammunition among them. Put double sentries at every post. Board up every window, leaving only loopholes. Stack wagon beds around the powder magazine. Then see that the women and children are placed there."

The colonel was donning what battered, dented armor he could find. If the Sioux carried the walls, the last defense would be the magazine. Nobody said it, but it was a shared thought. If it came to the worst, the magazine would be blown up. The women and children wouldn't face capture, or probably worse, torture.

It wouldn't be enough; Portugee was certain of that. They had two things upon which to lean. The worsening weather might hold back the Sioux, or help would arrive from Laramie. That last was a futile prop. Laramie didn't even know they needed help. How long had they stared down the trail, hoping to see help on the way?

"Yes, sir." Ten Eyck whirled and trotted away.

"I'll give a hand with those wagon beds," Portugee said.

He labored with the men, dragging the wagon beds to the magazine. They stacked them three high, and the best that could be hoped from this defense was that it would be a delay to the Sioux. It wasn't an unassailable bulwark.

The hardest work couldn't keep a man warm. The bottom must be dropping out of the thermometer. Portugee wanted to get inside for a few minutes, but a sentry yelled that the snow was piling higher against the stockade walls.

Portugee volunteered for a squad sent out to shovel away the drifts. He was appalled at the height the drifts had reached in such a short time. The wind had blown it into fantastic heights, and in several places, they were high enough so that a man could climb them and drop over the walls. Out here, the fiendish wind slashed at men until they couldn't take more than fifteen-minute shifts. No matter how hard a man worked, he couldn't get even the illusion of warmth. The wind-driven cold burned his lungs and left him gasping.

He was glad to turn over his shovel to his relief and step

inside where the protection of the walls blunted the wind's teeth.

Lanterns could only make a faint nimbus of light, and a few feet from them there was only the swirling grayness. More than the gloom of this weather bore down on a man; the gloom of his thoughts added a far heavier burden.

He hurried to the sutler's to get warm. He wanted heat both inside and outside. He ordered whiskey and downed it without thinking of its usual raw burning. It tasted as cold as a wintry, mountain stream, and he was beginning to believe he wasn't going to get its usual inward burning, either, then the warmth spread its tendrils throughout him.

It wasn't the lack of usual business that made Lyford so pasty-faced. Fear had him in its grip and was shaking him to pieces. Portugee felt no sympathy for him. Hell, every man in Fort Phil Kearny knew that.

He ordered another drink, wishing he could linger with it, but it was getting close to the time when a shoveler wanted somebody to relieve him.

Kathy came over to him, and her eyes were enormous in a bloodless face. "It's bad, isn't it, Portugee?"

He could think of nothing to assure her. By this time, the news of the disaster had to be all over the fort. The repeating of talk usually swelled it out of proportion, but in this case, exaggeration couldn't make it much worse.

"Yes," he said flatly.

He saw the glistening shine of moisture in her eyes, and he was afraid she was going to break into tears. "Here now," he said awkwardly.

"Have you seen Tom?"

He shook his head, thinking that Hutson would be occupied by a thousand chores.

"He'll be in when he can, Kathy."

"I'm not afraid," she cried. "But we had so little. If only—" Color flooded her face, and she stopped.

He knew what she meant. She was thinking of the lost time and was resentful that they had been denied it.

He patted her shoulder with a clumsy hand. "You've got to quit thinking that way. Something will happen—" He stopped helplessly. What it could be, he didn't know.

He looked back at her from the door. Her face was turned toward him, but she didn't see him. This post knew its grieving women for one reason or another but all of it bringing its misery.

He put in two more shifts on the shoveling, and as slow as it seemed, they had made some progress. Some of that awesome height of the drifts had been cut down. It would have to be done all over again. The damned snow and wind would see to that.

It was time to see Mrs. Wheatley, and the dread of it had made him put it off as long as he could. He still didn't know what he was going to say to her. He hadn't yet seen Mrs. Grummond, and maybe the dread of that was even worse. She had a double reason, and seeing a woman break down always left him feeling so helpless.

The kids said Hattie was with Mrs. Wheatley, and he hugged them fiercely. The boy struggled free and asked, "Are we in bad trouble?"

"Where did you hear that?"

"I heard some of the soldiers talking. Pa, were a lot of the soldiers killed?"

"Just soldier talk, son. Don't either of you go outside. Unless somebody tells you to. Then you do just what they say. Mama will be back soon."

They nodded solemnly, their eyes bright with interest. They weren't old enough to know fear of something that might happen. Portugee thought that every adult, on the post, would trade places with them.

He took a deep breath before he knocked on the Wheatley door. Hattie let him in, and though her face was drawn, her eyes were calm enough.

"Hot coffee's ready, John."

What a blessing she was. She didn't ask him fool questions that he couldn't answer.

He sat down across the table and reached out to cover Mrs. Wheatley's hand. She tried to give him a smile, but it wasn't true. She knew. He didn't have to tell her.

Her eyes had a hollow, vacant look. They didn't show any evidence of hard crying, but that was all inward, the kind that ripped a person to pieces.

She made it more simple for him. "You found him, didn't you, Portugee?"

He nodded gravely.

"They wouldn't let me see him." That despairing cry was wrung from her.

He would never forget how Wheatley looked. It was best that she didn't. He gave her the only consolation he could find.

"It was quick and easy."

That didn't mean much to her now. She went back to that vacant staring.

He drank his coffee and stood. Hattie walked to the door with him.

"See if you can get her over to our place."

Her quick understanding was there. "Yes, John."

"I don't know what I'll be doing. If somebody comes after you, go with them."

She searched his face, and for a moment, she was breathless. "Yes, John," she repeated.

He stepped out into the bitter cold. Quite a few men were going to the stables, and he joined them.

"What's up," he asked a man.

The man shook his head. "The colonel wants everybody to assemble there."

The stables cut off the wind; they couldn't stop the cold. Portugee thought that every man was there, except for the ones too sick to walk. He looked at Powell and Hutson, and Powell gave him a small shake of his head. Powell didn't know either, why this was called.

Carrington's appearance stopped the murmur of talk. Men

136

watched him with apprehensive eyes. It had to be something drastic for Carrington to call everybody out like this.

Carrington's head was bowed for a moment; it could be prayer, or a last marshaling of his thoughts. His eyes swept over them again, and he said, "All of you know our dismal plight. We cannot hold out unless we get aid. Fort Laramie is the nearest place from which we can expect it. And they won't come unless they know what we are facing. I need a volunteer to carry a dispatch."

Portugee heard the faint shuffling of men's feet, but none of them spoke out. That had been tried before, and they knew what those results had been.

"I'll try, sir." Hutson stepped forward.

A collective sigh ran through all of them, of relief and doubt.

Carrington stared at him with brooding eyes, and for a dreadful moment, Portugee thought the colonel would accept Hutson's offer. But Hutson hadn't enough experience to get through.

Carrington shook his head before he spoke. "No, Mr. Hutson." The tone of his voice softened his refusal. "You do not know the trail well enough."

His eyes moved from face to face. Not a man spoke or moved. Portugee didn't expect any of them to; unless it was Bridger. But Bridger looked as though he was carved out of stone.

Portugee stepped forward. "I'll go, sir." He knew the trail, and God knew he had enough motivation.

Some of the tension seemed to drain out of Carrington. "Yes, Mr. Phillips. I'll need an hour to write my dispatches."

Portugee checked him before he could turn away. "One other thing. I'll need Gray Eagle."

Was that a slight hesitation in Carrington? Portugee thought so. Turning over a favorite horse to another man would cost a man a sharp thrust of remorse.

"Of course, Mr. Phillips. He will be ready." The words were said strongly enough.

CHAPTER EIGHTEEN

Powell and Hutson stopped Portugee before he left the stables. "We're going with you," Powell said fiercely. Hutson's stern face gave full indication of how he felt.

Portugee shook his head. "I'm going alone." Just taking care of himself was more than he wanted.

"What if you're attacked," Hutson cried.

"Do you think three would do much better than just one," Portugee replied.

Hutson's face fell. He didn't have to answer.

"Portugee, let me know what I can do," Powell said.

"Sure." Portugee didn't look back.

He had many things to do in that hour. He wanted to spend a few minutes with Hattie, and his preparation would take some time.

Hattie knew something was happening without him speaking about it. There was that knack of reading his thoughts again.

He did not try to soften it. "I'm riding for help, Hattie. I'll follow the main trail to Fort Reno and then on to the wireless operation at Horseshoe Station. Perhaps we can get some help from the garrison at Fort Reno. If not, the telegram from Horseshoe to Laramie will bring what we need. Don't worry, I'll get through."

Her face whitened, and she closed her eyes but only for an instant.

"What can I do, John?"

He didn't have to tell her there was no other way. "I'll need all the clothes I can put on. And some food, too."

He refused her suggestion of sandwiches. They would be too bulky, and only a few of them wouldn't carry him through.

"I have some biscuits from last night's supper."

"That'll do it," he said. He could fill the outer pockets with them.

He put on a double layer of clothes, including socks. He had to struggle to pull his buffalo boots over his regular ones. He donned his buffalo coat, and he smiled with no real mirth. In a few minutes time, he had grown to bear-size in appearance.

She came to him and hugged him tightly, and all of her yearning was in it. She stepped back and tried to smile.

"You be careful," she said.

"Sure," he answered. She had gotten the kids into bed, and they were asleep. He stood over them a long moment, not touching them. He came back and picked up his Henry. He didn't look at her as he left.

He leaned against the wind as he walked by the colonel's office. He didn't see a light. That probably meant Carrington was waiting for him at the stables.

His breathing was faster as he reached them. He had on too damned many clothes. He wouldn't have after he left the fort. He hadn't seen a thermometer, but he would bet it was down to twenty-five degrees below zero.

"The colonel is waiting at the water gate," a private said. "Gray Eagle is saddled."

That was good. "Did anybody think of grain for the horse?"

"The saddlebags are filled." The man hesitated. He clearly had something else he wanted to say.

Portugee waited, but the man didn't speak. He was glad he didn't try.

Four men waited for him at the water gate, Carrington, a sergeant, and two privates. Portugee was just as happy there were no more. He would detest a big gathering to see him leave. One of the privates held Gray Eagle, and the thorough-bred danced his displeasure at being led out into the severe cold.

Carrington handed Portugee a thin, wrapped package. "Two telegrams to be sent from Horseshoe Station. One to General Cooke, at Omaha, the other to General Grant, in Washington."

Portugee's face didn't change. Carrington was going all the way to the top.

"Have Horseshoe Station send another one to General Palmer, at Laramie. Inform him that we need immediate help. There is also a dispatch for Colonel Wessells at Fort Reno requesting all the assistance he can provide. Tell him how desperate we are, but tell him not to jeopardize his own position. He is probably as understaffed as we are. But perhaps he can be of help to you."

Portugee nodded and tucked the thin packet into an inner pocket. It would not be taken out until he reached Fort Reno.

He swung up, and the sergeant's shoulder went under his butt and boosted him. The help was welcome. All of these clothes were pretty encumbering. He reined the horse down, and it danced in a little circle. The trail would take that out of him.

He looked around, a last look at the fort. It looked like a deserted post. Outside of these men with him, he could see no one. Beyond him was only a gray, foreboding world, filled with snow, tossed about by the great hand of the wind.

One of the privates said what was on his mind. "You won't be able to see them very far in this."

Portugee gave him a laconic answer. "They won't be able to see me any farther."

Carrington reached up and grasped Portugee's gauntleted hand. "May God help you."

Portugee nodded. That said it all.

The sergeant unfastened the padlock, and the two privates pulled out the bars and opened the gate.

Portugee wheeled the horse and guided it through the gate. Its pace immediately picked up to a steady trot. Portugee thought he heard the gate close, but the wind made uncertain hearing any such small sounds.

Carrington's head was bent as he listened to the diminishing sounds of Gray Eagle's hoofs. "Good," he muttered, and he wasn't speaking to anybody in particular. "He's left the trail." It would make it harder to travel, but it would muffle the beat of a horse's hoof.

He listened until the last faint sound was wind-wiped away. He turned and walked back to his office, and his shoulders drooped.

The sergeant and a private closed and barred the gate.

CHAPTER NINETEEN

Portugee kept the thoroughbred to a steady trot, avoiding the heavier drifts whenever he could. Nothing took the strength quicker out of a horse, than bucking drifts. So far he had detected no distress in Gray Eagle's breathing. He judged he was several miles off of the trail, but he wasn't lost, which wasn't hard for a man to do in this storm. He knew this country almost as well as the Sioux did. He thought he had a stouthearted horse under him, though he had not yet asked for the final proof.

The weather should have driven every living thing to shelter hours ago. But he couldn't depend upon that. The Sioux were unpredictable. "And tough," he said aloud. "Don't forget that." The Sioux could survive rigors that would have beaten a man to his knees. A bare-limbed grove of trees could give them shelter against the wind, or a rocky bluff running the right way. A Sioux could go where a white man didn't dare venture.

"Except me," he said and grinned. "And I'm crazy."

The horse's ears pricked forward and backward as though the sound of a human voice carried its consolation to him.

Portugee reached forward and patted its neck. How far had he gone, he wondered. He stomped on that question. Horseshoe Station was a long way down the trail to even begin asking himself such questions.

He judged another hour had passed, and he swung off and led the horse. Both of them needed that; the horse to be relieved of his weight and him to restore circulation in his numbed feet and legs. Extreme cold was a treacherous thing. It crept into a man's bones, killing all feeling in his flesh before he realized it.

He took exaggerated strides, forcing the blood to run freely again. He walked at least a mile before he mounted again. He kept his mind blank of all the thoughts that would so cruelly flog him, if he allowed them. This pace seemed maddeningly slow, but he would not let impatience put an additional strain on him or the horse. This pace wouldn't cover very many miles in any one hour, but a night's travel would add up to an impressive total. He planned to travel only at night, hiding during the daylight hours in the densest thicket he could find. How many days would it take him to reach Horseshoe? He would not reflect upon that, either.

The gray dawn was a long time coming, and he hadn't yet found a thicket that suited him. Maybe the snowfall had lessened a little; the cold hadn't. He pressed on, thinking he would find the right thicket over the slope ahead.

A war whoop froze his blood, announcing that he was discovered. He searched half of the compass, behind him, before he saw them. They came at him on two tangents, and he would say there were twenty of them. By its size, it wasn't the usual war party. He would say it was probably a hunting party on the move with the coming of dawn. He debated a moment, then turned the horse and stopped it. He drew the Henry from its scabbard, discounting the loss of a few precious seconds against what it could gain him. The Indians were two or three hundreds yards away, and he had only a faint hope of hitting one, but he wanted them to know what he carried. He could put respect in them and make them more cautious, but it would not stop them.

He stripped off the clumsy outer gauntlet and tucked it under his coat. The cold immediately struck through the thin cotton glove. But it would keep the bare trigger finger from touching the frozen metal.

He aimed and fired three rapid shots. That let them know he carried one of those modern repeating rifles that they so dreaded. One of those shots must have been close for he saw several of them veer abruptly. It made one small change; they spread out, but he didn't stop.

He had no return fire from them, and that told him that none of them carried guns. He was far out of arrow range, and he couldn't let them get any closer. He didn't think of an arrow hitting him; his big concern was that one of them would graze the horse.

He whirled Gray Eagle and asked for proof of his superior speed. He had a bigger, taller horse than those undersized Indian ponies, and he wanted assurance that his longer legs were faster than the winter-starved ponies.

He kept looking behind him, and he could see the gap between him and them widen. He couldn't pick his course now, and he couldn't avoid all of the drifts. He leaped some of them and plowed through others. He could still hear the Indians' yelling, but it had a new note in it; rage and disappointment that he was drawing away from them.

He looked back again, and the Indians had diminished to dot size. He lessened his demands upon Gray Eagle to ease his labored breathing, but he could not stop. He reached the gap to a frozen creek bottom, and the creek ran in the right direction to prevent the wind from filling its banks with drifts. He turned down it, and the snow covered the slickness of the ice. It gave Gray Eagle purchase and after a few yards, Portugee quit worrying about his hoofs flying from under him.

He kept to the creek bed, and he could see nothing about him. That race should have spent the Indian ponies, but he could not relax on that.

He let Gray Eagle alternately trot and walk, and he stopped him where the ice looked thin. He dismounted and crashed his heel through the ice, and water bubbled out. He stretched out and drank, then let the horse drink. He had a small argument about dragging the animal away because it hadn't had enough, but he could not risk it foundering itself.

He mounted and scanned the country as far as he could see, but nothing moved in it to attract his attention. He had to find his hideup for the day, but it couldn't be around here.

He pushed on for another hour and found what he wanted; a brush-choked ravine at the top of a hill. From here, he could keep the country under view from all directions.

Gray Eagle was tired, but he wasn't suffering. Portugee rubbed his legs down with the big gauntlets. He had asked for solid proof and had received it, but he didn't want another race, like the last one at least, for a while.

He fed the horse grain out of his cupped hands and replenished it. Gray Eagle nickered for more, and Portugee said, "That's enough, boy." He stroked his muzzle, sorry that he had to keep him on skimpy rations.

He nibbled on a biscuit that was as cold and hard as a small stone. His hunger must not be very much for it satisfied him.

He spent the long, dragging day, walking Gray Eagle in circles in the ravine to keep both of their blood circulating. He would stop when he was leg-weary, and whenever he sat down, he dozed. He never slept longer than a few minutes. Each time, his uneasiness jerked up his head. A quick survey of the empty country reassured him, then he would get up and walk again in their cramped, hiding place. With the coming of dusk, he and Gray Eagle had the snow well-beaten down.

He waited until the dusk deepened, then he was in the saddle again. The snow had stopped, but the wind was as strong as ever. The cold was never as bad, if it wasn't wind driven. He would have given a lot, during the day, if he could have built a fire, even a small one to give its illusion of heat.

He thought he should reach Fort Reno sometime in the late night hours. He grinned mirthlessly at an errant thought. He was trying to make Fetterman's taunt come true; he was attempting to ride through the whole Sioux nation.

The only difference was that he didn't have seventy-nine men behind him. He was alone.

The night hours stubbornly gave way and he was beginning to think his sense of direction had betrayed him when he saw the dark bulk of Fort Reno looming up ahead of him. He had ridden sixty-seven miles, by the trail. He wouldn't even attempt to estimate how many more he had added to that.

He rode up to the gate, and a sentry challenged him. "Scout with message," Portugee shouted.

It seemed an interminable wait until the gates swung open. A soldier led him to the stables, and Portugee dismounted. God, every joint was stiff, and every step pulled a grunt from him.

He turned and came back to where the soldier held Gray Eagle. "Feed him light," he ordered. "I can't afford for him to be slowed down."

Men were racing toward him, and the man, in the lead, was the officer of the guard.

"Take me to Colonel Wessells," Portugee demanded.

The officer looked at him with disapproval. "The colonel is asleep."

"I don't give a good goddamn what he's doing," Portugee snapped. "I'm carrying bad news."

He locked eyes with the officer, and the man couldn't hold his eyes steady. "I'll have him awakened," the officer muttered.

Portugee waited in the colonel's office while the officer went to get him. At least, it was warm in here. He fought the heaviness of his eyes. A couple of times, his head dropped onto his chest, and the contact snapped his eyes open. Where was that damned colonel?

Colonel Henry Wessells came in, and sleep was still in his eyes.

"Dispatches from Fort Phil Kearny," Portugee said tersely.

That cleared Wessells' eyes. Portugee saw the tightening of his cheeks as he read Carrington's dispatch.

147

Wessells said incredulously, "You've ridden all the way from Fort Kearny?"

"Yes," Portugee said. Couldn't the man read?

"Colonel Carrington only states that he is in desperate need of help. He doesn't say why."

"He's lost half of his garrison. Captain Fetterman and seventy-nine men were massacred by the Sioux. The fort can't withstand a single assault by the Sioux."

Wessells' ruddy complexion whitened. "Good God," he whispered. "I can't send help. "I'm down to a bare roster. Sending aid to Colonel Carrington would only jeopardize holding both forts."

"We didn't expect it. I've got to get those other dispatches through to Horseshoe Station. Carrington expects help from Laramie."

"I can spare a man or two to go with you."

Portugee grinned bleakly at him. "I don't want them. A lone man can ride faster and hide better."

"My God, man. You can't go on tonight. You've got to get some sleep."

Portugee shook his head. "There's no time. I'll take some hot coffee and maybe eat a little." As for sleep he could do that during the daylight hours.

The mess sergeant served him hot coffee and slabs of cold roast beef. Portugee waved away the bread.

"Tell the stables I'll be ready to go in a half-hour. Have my horse ready."

He chewed away, and now the warmth was his enemy. It weakened a man, lulling him into sleep.

He shook himself, got up, and pulled on his heavy coat. He didn't have much of that half-hour left.

Wessells met him at the stables and handed him another dispatch. "Have that sent to General Palmer at Laramie."

Portugee nodded. Wessels couldn't add anything to what he already carried, but maybe it would strengthen it.

He swung up, and Wessells stared at him. Maybe he had a lot of words he wanted to say, but he kept it simple.

"Good luck."

"Sure," Portugee said. He had had a lot of it in getting here. He would need a lot more of it. The bulk of his ride was before him; one hundred and thirty miles to Horseshoe Station. And that was by the trail. He remembered how far he had to leave the trail to reach here. He wished he could count on it not being more than a hundred and thirty miles.

He raised a gauntleted hand in a final salute and turned Gray Eagle toward the gates. This was the twenty-second of December. Realization of the date filled him with dismay, then he overrode it. He couldn't do anything about it.

He wouldn't let himself look back at Fort Reno. It had been warm in there. The snow was falling again, and the wind had never stopped. He wanted to rave and swear at the weather. Something stung his face, and he waited a minute until he was sure. That tears it, he thought bitterly. It was sleeting.

CHAPTER TWENTY

He could not let his sense of urgency push the horse beyond its endurance, and every drift was pulling on the animal's strength. He could not go around some of them. In places, he bucked drifts five feet high. Several times, he dismounted and tramped down a path through the worst of them, walking back and forth. It drained the strength from his legs until they were trembling, but it made it easier for Gray Eagle. He could give the walking only one thing; it forced life back into his frozen legs, and he felt the fierce fire of returning circulation.

This is the twenty-third, he thought as dawn filtered its feeble light through the merciless storm. The sleeting hadn't stopped. He was pelleted and buffeted from every angle, and he accepted it with dull resignation. He had cursed it until he was empty of oaths, and searching for more wouldn't be worth the effort.

It was full daylight, but he kept on. He was well aware that the stronger light brought additional danger to him, but the passing time was a savage prod. How many miles had he covered now? He couldn't add it up. His dulled thoughts couldn't focus on anything for long. But he should be past the threat of roving war parties.

He went on through the brutal hours, riding and walking. When he rode, a plodding horse chewed at the endless miles. When he trudged, he led a weary horse. He was killing this noble animal, and he couldn't stop it.

The thickening dusk brought his first awareness that the

day was ending. He was somewhere north of the Platte, and surely, he could stop for an hour's rest. It wasn't his choice to make; both animal and man had to have it.

He jerked to rigid attention as he heard that chilling war whoop again. Oh God, he should be beyond that danger. Gray Eagle was no longer fresh; he couldn't outrun even the starved Indian ponies.

He located the war party behind him, and he couldn't count them, but they were more than he could cope with, and he couldn't outrun them. His eyes searched frantically for nearby shelter, but that alone wouldn't do him any good. They would search it until they flushed him out.

He saw a small, conical hill that rose abruptly from the plains, and he headed for it. It was no more than a half mile away, and he had to make a monstrous demand upon a horse that had already been called on for too much.

It gamely responded, but he knew it could not keep up that run for too long. He looked back, and he wasn't drawing away as he had done the first time he had been jumped.

Just make the hill, Gray Eagle, he prayed. You'll have a long rest there. The hills' height would give him command of all sides. The Indians would have to climb it to get at him, and the Henry would change their minds. If he could hold it until nightfall, the Indians would drop their attack until the morning's light. An Indian didn't do his fighting at night for the gods of evil walked about in the dark hours.

The horse was blowing hard by the time it reached the crest. Portugee jumped off, and it was a barren area, not much bigger than enough for a horse and man to occupy. Gray Eagle stood with drooping head, and that was a bad sign of approaching exhaustion.

He pulled out the Henry and snugged it to his shoulder. The foremost Indians weren't much beyond a hundred yards away. They might have even gained on him a little. Their mouths were stretched with their yelling, and Portugee shut his mind to it.

He drew his bead and pulled the trigger. He had no more

time than to note that an Indian tumbled from his pony before he was seeking a new target. He fired three more times and plucked off three more riders.

They whirled their ponies and split as they galloped madly back, and the range was too long. He lowered the rifle and waited, breathing hard. That wouldn't stop them; it only made them retreat until they talked over a new method of attack.

Whatever they planned to do would have to be fast before full night caught them.

They separated before they came within range, and half of them made a wide swing to take the hill from the rear.

He drove the ones before him back with two well aimed shots, then whirled to cover his rear. He got one and missed another, but it must have been close by the way the Indian swerved his pony and raced away, the others following him.

They gathered together, well beyond his reach, and he knew the furious words they must be hurling at each other. The night deepened, and he couldn't see them any longer. But they were out there. Now he would find out, if Indians ever attacked at night.

He sank on his haunches and peered into the blackness. He couldn't see a damned thing. He would have to depend upon his ears, and the wind wasn't a friend to them.

A man couldn't keep track of true time in this situation, and he knew his estimate of how long it had been was probably false.

He sighed, and there was no shock in what he saw. The small campfires ringed the hill. They had no intention of leaving. With the morning light, they could pick up their quarry at their leisure.

Gray Eagle's head was lifted, and Portugee could have sobbed with relief. The rest had done the horse a world of good. He fed him cupped handfuls of grain, and the horse ate, which was a farther good sign.

He moved about the hilltop, checking first one direction, then another. He had two things to fight now; the cold and his weariness. He dared not close his eyes, not even for the briefest dozing, for if he did, he could very well not awake again. The best way to avoid that was to stay on his feet, moving about the interminable beat of his little circle. Those campfires mocked him, and he could imagine how his hands would feel spread out to one of them.

He forced those stiffening legs into one step, then another. Fantastic thoughts tortured him. Maybe tomorrow's light would never come; maybe he was forever doomed to walk a circle that had no beginning, no ending.

The slow hours dragged away. If he was right about Indian behavior, they would attack at dawn in the first true light of the morning. He waited for the false dawn, the faint light that might awaken a man but put no inclination in him to crawl out of his blankets. He would be in the saddle, hoping to slip through the Indian line before any of them were fully awake.

That faint streak of gray in the eastern sky finally came. He mounted and kept Gray Eagle to a slow walk down the slope. He could see no campfires now; they had been allowed to go out in the late hours of the night. Each cautious step strung him tighter. He hoped to slip through those sleeping Indians without awakening any of them.

He rode with the Henry across his lap, and the heavy gauntlet was tucked inside his coat. The increasing tension actually made his breathing painful. He did not want to ask this tired, gaunt horse for another run, and he prayed the need wouldn't rise.

Dark, huddled forms were on both sides of him now, and he was going to make it. Then one of the huddled forms threw aside its blankets and rose to its feet. Did some ancient instinct waken the Indian, or had he heard some small sound that reached through the unconsciousness of sleep? Portugee didn't know, but the figure was leaping at him.

He pulled the trigger without raising the rifle, and the muzzle flame was almost in the Indian's face. The face fell away, and Portugee asked Gray Eagle for that run. The reach of those long legs was missing now, but Gray Eagle gave the best he had. Behind him, Portugee thought he heard the startled cries, the confused sounds of men asking what had happened. The darkness still held, and Portugee doubted the Indians would make any move until the light came.

He kept the horse at that run until he thought he caught a weaving in him, then eased the reins. He listened and heard nothing above the wind. The Indians were waiting for light, and by that time, he should be well away from them.

He let the horse walk and kept to the trail this time. He could not afford an extra mile. He did not voice his cursing words, but he thought the words. In all his life, he had never seen a winter this bitter.

Surely, he would not run into another Indian party. He had thought that last evening, but he was so much nearer Laramie. Another war party couldn't be operating this close.

He hadn't eaten in a long time, and he reached for a biscuit. He looked at the frozen, hard lump, and the effort, to gnaw on it, was too much. He slipped it back in his pocket.

The relentless miles fell slowly behind him. He didn't know exactly where he was, but he should be getting close to the North Platte. Horseshoe Station was just beyond the river.

A cry choked in his throat at the appearance of two horsemen. Dear God! He couldn't face it again. He could not ask Gray Eagle for another burst of speed. It could too easily kill the horse. If Gray Eagle could give it, where would Portugee run to? The two horsemen were in front of him, blocking the trail to Horseshoe. He cleared the Henry and waited. With each approaching step, a conviction grew in him. They weren't Indians, they were white men; he could tell by the way they rode.

He hailed them, and his voice was a croaking rasp. He hadn't tried to use it for too long. He rose in the stirrups and waved frantically at them, and they returned it.

He let their increased pace cut down the distance between them. He recognized one of them as they drew near. It was Captain Bailey, a leader of a mining group in the area. Portugee didn't know where Bailey had gotten the title, but he was a civilian. He didn't know the other.

Portugee didn't attempt a smile of greeting. His face was still from the cold, and he had the feeling that if he moved it, it would crack into a thousand pieces.

Bailey introduced George Dillon. Portugee had heard of him. He was a rancher and wagon train boss. Both of them were tough men. They had to be to live even in this relatively safe area.

"How far am I from Horseshoe?" Portugee's voice needed greasing.

"Not far. The North Platte's just ahead," Bailey answered. "Horseshoe Station is just beyond it."

Portugee should know that. He had traveled this trail often enough, but he was so damned tired that he couldn't get hold of a solid thought.

"What are you doing out here, Portugee?" Bailey asked. "Did you ever see a worse goddamned winter?"

That almost made Portugee try to grin and crack his face. Who knew it worse than him. "I've got to get dispatches to Horseshoe. Fort Kearny has had a massacre. Carrington can't hold without help."

They exchanged startled looks, and Bailey said, "You didn't come clear from Kearny?"

Portugee nodded, too tired to furnish any details.

"Good God," Dillion exclaimed in astonishment. "The Sioux must be out."

"Yes," Portugee said simply.

"Then you must've seen some of them."

Portugee nodded grimly.

"We'll ride back to Horseshoe with you," Bailey said. He and Dillon turned their horses.

Portugee was grateful for the company. It was good to see a friendly face and hear the right language.

Bailey wanted to step up the pace, and Portugee shook his head. "I can't go any faster."

Bailey really looked at Gray Eagle for the first time. "Say! That horse looks done in."

"He is." Portugee made no further explanation. Nobody needed to be told just how bad a shape Gray Eagle was in.

They crossed the frozen North Platte at Bridger's ferry, and Horseshoe Station was just ahead. Portugee almost fell as he dismounted, and it took several steps to even begin to restore the circulation.

He led Gray Eagle to the lee of the log building. He wished he had better shelter for him. He turned toward the door of the building, and he moved like an old man, each step making his legs scream with agony. He was here; he had made it.

CHAPTER TWENTY-ONE

He walked into the telegraph office, and the operator looked at him with rounded eyes. The pot-bellied stove was a glowing red, and Portugee staggered to it.

"I've got dispatches from Kearny," Portugee said. His voice still wasn't normal. "Wait until I get my hands thawed out so I can use my fingers."

He heard Dillon and Bailey telling the operator the sketchy details they knew. He thought he smelled the singeing of hair. Hell, that buffalo coat was right up against the stove.

He moved back, setting his teeth against the agony the heat was causing. He didn't have blood in his veins any more; in its place was millions of fiery-pointed needles. Drops of water were beginning to drip from his ice-covered coat.

He stayed by the stove until his hands no longer felt like frozen chunks of meat. His fingers fumbled in his pocket and brought out the dispatches. He picked out the one written by Colonel Wessells.

"Send that to General Palmer at Laramie." Laramie had to send that help. Portugee wanted it on its way as quickly as possible.

He listened to the clacking of the key. Oh God, he was so tired. But he could rest now.

The operator finished sending, then tapped out a few more letters. His frown deepened. "I'm not sure they got that. I can't get a response from them. Maybe the wire's down, or they're not attending their key because of the holiday."

Portugee groaned. He had known wires to break under a

159

heavy coating of ice. He hated to admit the other possibility; that the Sioux had cut them.

His sluggish thoughts mulled over what the operator said at the last. Oh Jesus! The man said something about a holiday. This was Christmas, and he had forgotten all about it. He wasn't done; he wasn't sure that Laramie had received the plea for help for Kearny. He couldn't stop until he was certain.

He picked up the dispatches and put them back into his pocket. He had promised a lot of people, back there, that he would see that the dispatches were delivered. He hadn't done it yet.

"I can try again in an hour or two," the operator said.

Portugee shook his head. He could wait around here all that time with no assurance of raising Laramie.

Bailey read his face. "You can't go, Portugee. Laramie's forty miles. You're already half-froze."

"Not as bad as I was," Portugee said. "What time is it?"

The operator looked at his watch. "Going on eleven."

Portugee nodded. He could still make it before the day was gone.

Bailey tried a last argument. "That horse can't make it."

Portugee could read faces too, and refusal was in Bailey's and Dillon's eyes. They had no intention of offering their horses, and Portugee wouldn't have asked them. They had someplace to go, and maybe somebody waited for them. Not with the anxiety of other people, he thought wearily, but he didn't say it.

He looked at all of them before he closed the door behind him.

What could he say to a horse that had already given too much? He offered him the last of the grain, and Gray Eagle refused to eat. Portugee sighed and hoisted himself into the saddle. That step to the stirrup was higher, than he remembered it.

He kept to that slow, dogged walk, and at times he could swear he was making no progress. He lost sense of time, of feeling, of anything. He had sunk into a lethargy, barely aware of the passing of the hours. He walked for stretches until his legs rebelled, then climbed up again. He no longer agonized over the slowness of the miles. He clung to one single thought; he had to get to Laramie.

He was grateful for the lessening of the light. Night would come swiftly, but that meant so many miles were behind him. How much was left? He didn't have the slightest idea.

He kept peering ahead, trying to see the darker mass of Fort Laramie. Gray Eagle was weaving, and Portugee could feel the trembling in his body. This wasn't caused by the cold; this was caused by sheer exhaustion.

He had to push on; there was no other alternative.

A sentry stared out over the walls at a slow-moving mass of ice and snow. It had appeared through a rent in the curtain of snow, and it couldn't be a man and horse.

He watched it a moment longer, and his eyes verified what he refused to believe. It was a horseman, both man and animal apparently in bad shape. The man was slumped forward, and the horse moved with stumbling steps, looking as though it was barely able to drag its hoofs along.

"Who goes there?" he challenged.

The answering voice was a feeble, hoarse croak, and the sentry had to strain to hear it.

"Scout from Fort Kearny. With urgent dispatches for General Palmer."

The sentry bawled for the officer of the guard. This couldn't be a trick, for only one horseman was out there, but who could believe that story about riding from Kearny?

An officer ran up, and the sentry relayed what he had heard. "He claims to be from Fort Kearny, sir. In this weather?" His question expressed his doubt.

"Open that gate," the officer snapped.

A lifetime passed while Portugee waited for the gates to open. He couldn't believe he was here, and he forced himself to sit straighter. Gray Eagle weaved as he stood.

Men ran out toward him, and an officer said, "Did you come from Kearny? Why that's two hundred and—"

"Yes," Portugee said dully. He knew how far it was. "Take me to General Palmer. We've had a massacre—"

He shook his head at the officer's flood of questions. He would only tell it all to Palmer. He doubted he had enough strength to go over it again.

The officer took hold of Gray Eagle's bridle and led him into the fort. The horse stumbled with every step. The officer had to slow his stride, for even a man's normal pace was too hard for the animal.

Portugee stayed in the saddle. Getting down and walking across the parade ground would be too much to ask him.

Gray Eagle was swaying definitely with each step, and his head hung low. Portugee slid to the ground. Maybe even this little bit of relief might have come too late.

"He's falling," the officer cried.

Portugee could see it. Gray Eagle listed far to one side, then regained his balance. But his legs were buckling. They no longer could hold him up. That great heart had nothing left.

He fell heavily, making no sound, not even the sigh of escaping breath.

The officer bent over him. "He's dead," he announced.

Portugee briefly closed his eyes. He didn't need the officer's words. He had known for hours that it was coming. Gray Eagle was dead before he hit the snow-covered ground.

He stood there, his head bent, and so many things filtered through his mind. He would never ride a better horse.

He looked up, and a lighted building was only a few yards away. Gray Eagle had almost carried him the last step.

He heard strains of music coming from the lighted building, and the officer felt as though some explanation was necessary.

"It's the bachelor officers' quarters. We call it Old Bedlam. They're holding a ball to celebrate Christmas."

Portugee absently nodded. The strains of the music picked

at him, and he finally recognized it. He should; he had heard "O Susanna" often enough. He thought of other people who would not be merry-making.

"You better get me to General Palmer," he said. If he stood here much longer, he would collapse like Gray Eagle did.

"He's attending the ball," the officer said hesitantly. "But I'll take you to him."

Portugee had barely enough strength to walk into the building.

The door of the brightly lighted room was opened, and the heat wrapped around Portugee. He wondered why the music had stopped, then he saw the reason. Officers, in their best uniforms, were chosing partners for the next dance from the fashionably gowned ladies.

The rush of frigid air into the room turned all heads toward him. They saw an awesome apparition, bundled up far beyond normal size. It dripped water as it stood there.

Several officers were frowning at this rude interruption.

"General Palmer," Portugee said. "I've got to see him."

A gray-haired man, with stars on the shoulders of his uniform, came after the others. The officers parted to give him passage.

"What is this? Who are you?" the general demanded.

Portugee felt dizzy, and the heat had heavy fingers, pulling at his eyelids. He could not keep his eyes open much longer.

"From Kearny," he said. "I must talk to you."

Palmer's eyes made their quick appraisal. "Come to my office."

"Jackson." Palmer picked out an officer. "Come with us."

Portugee trudged beside Palmer toward another building, forcing himself to take just one more step, then another.

He sank into a chair in Palmer's office without invitation, and he couldn't help it. In another second, he would pitch on his face.

My God, the effort it took to take the dispatches out of his pocket. It seemed as though a cloud of blackness was gathering just beyond the light, readying to make its rush at him.

"Dispatched from Colonel Carrington and Colonel Wessells," he said in that dog-tired voice. "Kearny had a massacre."

He heard Palmer's indrawn suck of breath, then Palmer was reading the messages. The blackness had moved in a little closer. If Palmer wanted more details, he had better hurry, or Portugee wouldn't be able to tell him.

Palmer looked up from his reading. "Carrington doesn't say anything about a massacre."

"Wessells does." Portugee had to drag out the words. "I saw it right after it happened. Captain Fetterman and seventy-nine men."

"All of them?" Palmer said incredulously.

"Not a man was alive." Portugee thought that somebody other than himself was talking. The words sounded so indistinct and far away.

He had to say something else, to make Palmer understand just how bad it was. "Half of Carrington's force was wiped out. Kearny cannot stand alone."

He wanted to add more, but he couldn't. He was sliding out of his chair, and he couldn't check it. From out of the onrushing blackness, he thought he heard somebody say, "This man needs help."

CHAPTER TWENTY-TWO

Portugee opened his eyes and winced as the light hurt them. He closed them against it. That was full daylight. He had slept through the rest of the night.

He opened his eyes again, and Palmer stood beside his bed. "How do you feel?"

Portugee grimaced. He felt like hell. He didn't have an ounce of flesh that didn't ache, and his feet and hands tingled and burned. "I slept longer than I thought."

"Do you know what day this is?"

"It has to be the twenty-sixth. I got here around midnight yesterday."

Palmer shook his head. "You rode in at eleven o'clock the twenty-fifth. Today is the twenty-seventh."

That stunned Portugee. He had slept an entire day plus a sizable chunk of another. He tried to sit up, and it was too much of an effort.

"General, you got those dispatches on the wire?"

Palmer nodded. "I sent Carrington's and one of my own to General Cooke yesterday morning. I've heard from him. I am to send two companies of cavalry and four of infantry to the relief of Fort Kearny."

Portugee stared in disbelief. He must have heard that wrong. Surely, that relief was gone. "It's already on its way?" He couldn't believe it. Palmer was shaking his head.

Portugee tried again and sat up. "My God," he exploded. "Those people are waiting for you." Hattie was waiting and

Mrs. Wheatley. Yes, and Mrs. Grummond. He could make it a long list.

"Wait until you look outside," Palmer said drily. "I had to wire General Cooke that the worst storm I've ever seen is raging. Visibility is cut down to a few yards. Men and equipment cannot be moved in such a storm. No man could get through."

Portugee's eyes blazed. He could have pointed out that he had, but he held his tongue. He hoped Palmer's estimation of complete immobility included the Sioux.

The accusation in Portugee's eyes scored Palmer. "Damnit, I'm having every possible preparation made. We will be ready to move the moment the storm eases."

Portugee sank back, and he was exhausted. One man, getting through wouldn't face Palmer's problems. Palmer had to move several hundred men and arrange the myriad details that attended it.

"Mr. Phillips, I think I understand what you feel. Believe me, I'd shut off this storm if I could."

Portugee nodded in weary resignation. "I want you to keep one thing in mind. When the troops move, I'm going with them."

"If you are able." Palmer threw cold water on that. "The post surgeon checked you over yesterday. You've suffered frostbite."

"How much?" Portugee asked harshly. He had seen the results of extreme frostbite. A man lost toes and fingers to prevent gangrene.

Palmer guessed at his thoughts. "The surgeon doesn't think it's bad. He will check you over again today. Man, haven't you done enough?"

Portugee didn't answer that. It wouldn't be enough until he saw Kearny standing intact.

His eyes were closing again. Hadn't he had enough sleep? He didn't hear Palmer slip quietly out of the room.

It was the next day before Portugee was able to hobble around. The surgeon frowned at such early activity, but

Portugee insisted. He had to see for himself Palmer's opinion of the weather.

He stepped out into a world smothered under snow, and it was still falling. Some of the drifts inside the fort were four feet high, and he could imagine what they would be like outside. Men did only what was necessary outside, and that was done as fast as possible. Paths were beaten down from building to building, and when the traffic ceased, the snow went back to work, refilling the paths. He could not argue with Palmer's words about his immobility. Everything was paralyzed by the storm. Portugee could draw on only one small hope. This would force the Sioux to huddle in their lodges. If they had not already taken Kearny, they would not do it until this ended.

He hobbled to the mess hall and back to his room. It was his only break in the hours of anguished waiting. He ate solitary meals, wanting neither company nor conversation. But he did notice that nearby officers stared as blankly at the walls as he did.

Would the Sioux get word that Palmer's relief column was coming? Portugee conceded the possibility of it. Enough of the so-called tame Sioux were camped within sight of the fort. Logic wiped that fear away. Even if some of them wanted to curry favor with Red Cloud, they could not travel in this weather.

The snowstorm raged into the new year of 1867, and the official temperature was reported to be 23.5 degrees below zero. Portugee couldn't argue with that. A few minutes outside was all the proof a man needed. He would not let himself think about Hattie and the kids. That raised questions he couldn't answer. He had to believe they were all right.

Palmer came to him on January first. "The weather seems to be lifting. We hope to move tomorrow. Do you still insist upon going?"

The shine in Portugee's eyes was enough answer. His feet still ached, but he was walking better.

Major James Van Vost commanded the relief column, four hundred men, well-armed and equipped. The Army let Portugee have his pick of the horses, but no matter how hard he looked, he would not find another Gray Eagle. But this bay would do. It would be a far easier trip for the bay, than it had been for Gray Eagle. The demands, Gray Eagle had known, wouldn't be put on the bay.

The wagons carried enough hay for ten days, and that should be enough. The struggle started the moment the column stepped outside, for there were no well-beaten paths such as those inside the fort. Portugee looked at an unfamiliar world. The wind had piled the snow to fantastic heights, obliterating the familiar landmarks. This wasn't going to be any picnic, either.

The infantry had to buck the drifts on foot, and Portugee pitied the poor devils. Vast snowdrifts stretched endlessly before them, too many of them six feet high. A man sank until he was waist deep, then the tremendous effort was repeated again. He had to lift his weight out of the soft, clinging mass, then force his leg foreward to take another step. All of that effort gained him such a little distance.

Portugee's scowl increased before they had gone a mile. The struggle was exhausting the men. He saw it in their strained faces and heard it in their panting breath. Something had to be done to make their walking easier, or they would be done long before they reached Fort Phil Kearny.

Van Vost saw it too. He sent the cavalry ahead to break trail for the infantry. Horsemen pushed ahead in file for a short distance, then countermarched over the same stretch to further trample down the snow. The infantry moved much better, but now the terrible strain had been transferred to the horses.

Cavalrymen cursed their mounts, kicking and flogging them into the drifts. Animals flung their heads, and their eyes rolled wildly as they put their weight behind their chests, fighting the unmovable mass of white. When the lead horsemen in the file broke through, the others followed with more ease. The leading horse had to be changed often, for a few minutes against these drifts drained them. It was working, a path was beaten down, but my God, how torturously slow it was. The footmen followed without the former difficulty.

Portugee rode in some of those trail-breaking files, and it didn't take too much of it to put a tremble in a horse's legs and a harsh tearing sound in their breathing.

Even the cavalry's effort couldn't break a path wide enough to keep the wagons rolling. In too many places shovels had to scoop the snow out of the way.

Portugee sat beside Van Vost, watching the crawling progress with brooding eyes.

Van Vost's face was harried, and he must have sensed Portugee's criticism. "Damn it," he exploded, then caught himself. "Can you think of anything better?" His tone had a strident note.

Portugee wasn't blaming him. Blame couldn't be put on a single man. "No," he said. He wished he could think of something better.

The day stretched out into a succession of nightmarish hours, and nobody regretted seeing the light go. Men sank down around campfires, slumping in near stupor. Many of them ate little, or none at all. That wasn't hard to understand. What they had put out today left little hunger in a man.

Portugee spread his blankets near a fire. At least, a man could know semblance of warmth from the fire. He stared at the sky and saw a star here and there. The cloud cover must be thinning. It looked as though tomorrow might be fair. He bitterly cursed the weather. An improvement in it was coming too late; the damage had already been done.

Sleep was a long time in coming. The question of how far they had come against how far they had to go crowded sleep out of his mind. Tomorrow would bring no cessation in the toil. He went to sleep with that big problem in his mind.

Every man, in this relief column, would never forget these

days. Drinking water was hard to find, and only by chopping through the ice in deepest holes could they get any at all. The buckets lowered into the hole came up dripping, and the water froze on the buckets encrusting them in hard, little pellets. The buckets were hand-chained to the waiting horses and mules, and it hurt Portugee each time he looked at the gaunted animals. The flesh had melted off of them until their bones could be easily traced.

Portugee shook his head at the small amount of hay remaining in the wagons. They had better be able to replenish it at Reno, he thought grimly.

He kept staring ahead of him, hoping to see Reno rise up before them. They had been on the trail eight horrible days. He would have to guess how many men were left in fighting condition. Too many men crippled about on frostbitten feet, and they would be fortunate, if toes were the only loss. He no longer worried about the Sioux. They would be too wise to be out in this. But then the Sioux didn't have the desperation driving them.

A grunt was all he could manage when Fort Reno came into view, but he knew a sweeping relief. Kearny was sixty-five miles away. He didn't attempt to figure how many days it would take to cover that distance.

It wasn't a smart Army formation that straggled through Fort Reno's gates. Van Vost tried to put some order into the weather-whipped men, and it couldn't be done. What did Van Vost expect, Portugee thought wearily; troops that looked as though they had just stepped off a parade ground?

Wessells stepped forward and wrung Portugee's hand. "I didn't expect to see you again," he confessed.

Portugee's grin wasn't very strong. "Several times I wasn't so sure myself."

"They look as though they've had a bad time."

"They've been through hell."

They spent the night there, and Portugee found no real rest. Once, he wouldn't have thought much of a mere sixty-five miles. Now it stretched out forever. His food sat sourly on his stomach, and it wasn't due to the quality of the meal. The miles before them would be no easier than the ones behind them. Harder, he thought, for all those hours were claiming their toll. They would have to leave men here to face amputation, and the horses were worn out. Worst, there was no hay at Fort Reno. The Army was going to lose a hell of a lot of horses, before this was over.

He was surprised to see Colonel Wessells come out in the morning. Wessells waited for his horse to be saddled, and he was dressed and packed for the trail. He looked unhappy. Wessells' going had to be because of official orders. Something had passed between Van Vost and him last night.

The rest of the hay ran out less than two days out of Fort Reno. Portugee looked at the horses and thought of the way Gray Eagle had staggered just before the end. Gray Eagle was stouter than any of these.

The emptiness in their bellies drove the horses, and they fought the picket line that night. Portugee watched the useless fight. The horses didn't have that kind of vitality left to waste it like this.

A sentry's bawling jerked him upright in his blankets. For a moment, a remembered fear gripped his throat. He had been wrong in thinking that the Sioux wouldn't be out in this.

He snatched up his rifle and ran toward the confusion. Men converged on it from all directions, and their blank, tight expressions told him they didn't know any more than he did.

Colonel Wessells was talking to the sentry when Portugee reached them.

"They're breaking their halter ropes, sir," the sentry said. "I'd say twenty are already loose. I just came up in time to see the last bunch go. Shall we go after them?"

Before Wessells could answer, another horse snapped its tether, and Portugee heard the small, sharp pop of the rope as it parted.

Wessells wearily shook his head. "At night, sentry? It

wouldn't do any good. Trying to find them would wear out the horses we have left."

Portugee was in full approval of Wessells' decision. Those horses were looking for grass, weeds, or leaves; anything to assuage the gnawing in their bellies. None of them would find anything. Any possible forage was covered by snow, and a horse wouldn't be able to paw down to it. A horse was an awkward animal when it came to using its hoofs for that purpose. A mule could get down through several inches, but this snow was too deep for even a mule.

He put sharpened attention on Wessells. Wessells issued the order instead of Van Vost. Something had happened back at Fort Reno. Was Wessells going to take over Carrington's command as well? Portugee remembered Wessells' unhappy expression before the command left Fort Reno. If Van Vost had handed him such orders, the displeasure of it mirrored in Wessells' face.

Portugee went back to his interrupted sleep, but it wouldn't return. He thought of a small gray man, buckling under one adverse happening after another. If Portugee's conjecture that Wessells was sent to take over Fort Phil Kearny, it meant that the Army had summarily judged Carrington and was replacing him. That order had to originate from Cooke. Portugee cursed him. Damn a higher headquarters that judged without knowing all of the facts.

He finally fell asleep thinking that the Army offered only a hard life, and sometimes an unfair one regardless of the rank.

The misery of the days increased. An abject command of men doggedly plowed on toward Fort Phil Kearny. Portugee saw the vivid red stains in footprints. Frostbite was striking harder. One man died by freezing, and hunger drove the horses crazy. They tried to chew splinters from the tongues of the wagons, and the empty feed troughs showed the scars from their nibbling teeth. Horses could not be tethered too close together, for they bit at the manes and tails of any other animal they could reach. Tails and manes were beginning to take on a scraggly look.

Portugee lost track of the passage of time. They had gone long beyond the normal stretch of days it should take to reach Fort Kearny. The hardships pounded at a man physically and mentally, and it was a small miracle that men didn't go stark mad under it.

He dully raised his head. A scout was trying to reach the command as fast as was possible, and the snow and his weakened horse was making slow, arduous work of it. Oh God! Were they facing an attack this far along?"

He saw the scout stop and talk with Wessells, and the news spread down the line. Animation erased the frozen misery of men's faces, and they were cheering. The scout had seen Fort Phil Kearny.

The hard lump in Portugee's throat made breathing difficult. At least, Fort Kearny still stood. The wretched, exhausted column tried to increase its pace, but it didn't matter much now.

The thirteen-day agony was over, for the gates of Fort Kearny were opening to receive them.

CHAPTER TWENTY-THREE

A staggering column passed through those gates, but men were trying to grin. People were lined on each side of the march, and Portugee anxiously searched for Hattie and the kids.

The lump expanded in his throat, and he wanted to cry. There they were! All three of them. He slid to the ground not caring where his mount went. He looked at her before his arms went around her. Her face was thinner, but the familiar shine was in her eyes.

"Hattie," he choked and held her hard. Neither of them spoke for a long moment, but they didn't need words. The feel of each other was answer enough.

She pulled back, and her eyes went over his face. "John, are you all right?"

"Fine, fine. All you all right?"

The radiance in her eyes could include a smile. "A little hungry and cold. There were some hours when I—" That small sigh was the only indication of how near she had been to the breaking point.

"Doubted that I'd come back?" he finished for her. "I had to," he said simply.

The kids yanked at his coat and clamored for attention. He picked them up, one in each arm. "Hush," he said. "It's all over." He held them tight, their cheeks pressed against his.

"Pa, you need a shave," his daughter protested.

"Pa, I'm hungry," his son complained.

Portugee could laugh freely and openly. He looked at the wagons trundling past them. Laramie had lavishly loaded them with everything needed.

"Why, we'll take care of both of those things right away." He tried to hold the three of them all at once, and he needed more arms.

All around them, people danced and shouted with joy. Hutson had Kathy in his arms, and they seemed to have blended into a single figure. Powell stood just beyond them, and his usual taciturn face was split in a broad grin.

Carrington stood talking to Wessells, and his face was grayer than Portugee remembered it. He looked like a man reeling under a brutal blow, and Portugee thought, Cooke is delivering the blow through Wessells. Carrington had put up a gallant effort, and it was coming to this.

Carrington turned his head, saw Portugee, and beckoned to him.

"The colonel wants me," Portugee said. "Jim's wife all right?"

"Yes," Hattie answered. "She was here just a moment ago." She looked around for her.

Perhaps Mrs. Wheatley had wanted to give them these few minutes alone. "I'll see her later," Portugee said.

He walked toward Carrington and Wessells.

Carrington's hard handclasp said everything that was in his heart. "Mr. Phillips, will you come into the office? There will be a change."

That unhappy look was back on Wessells' face. He hadn't wanted to be the messenger of that change.

Portugee walked into Carrington's office and took a chair at the colonel's invitation. Carrington slumped rather than sat down. He looked about at the familiar objects in the room as though they were strange to him. Was he trying to fix them in his mind?

Portugee's conviction grew. He knew without it being put into words. Carrington felt as though this was no longer his office.

Wessells sat on the edge of his chair, his eyes fixed on the floor.

"You came in good time," Carrington said. "We had no wood for heat except green cottonwood branches." His attempt at a smile was ghastly. "You know the poor heat they put out. We were almost out of vegetables. Scurvy was spreading. The post hospital was jammed with suffering victims. Only yesterday the surgeon told me that he wondered if the soldiers would just as soon die by scurvy as be scalped by the Sioux."

Portugee knew what Carrington was doing. He talked of important things but not the most important one to him.

Carrington's smile was like one painted on a wooden face. "The arrival of the horses puts us in an even more awkward situation. Colonel Wessells tells me that you have no hay. And we are out."

Wessells did not look up from the floor. "I'm sending a hundred and fifty horses back to Laramie," he muttered. "The mules will be turned out to forage as best as they can."

He lifted his eyes to Portugee, and the anguish was deep in them. It cried, what else can I do with them?

Portugee understood. Wessells wasn't asking him what to do about the horses. The detachment of soldiers who took the horses back might get to Laramie, but the horses wouldn't. In their half-starved condition, they would give out before they began to cover those miles. The Bozeman Trail would be marked by their bones for years.

Carrington's long, weary sigh sounded as though it tore him apart. He said what bore down so heavily on both officers.

"Colonel Wessells brought me orders. He is replacing me. I am to take command of Fort Casper."

It confirmed Portugee's conviction, but he said explosively, "No."

Carrington's face was a bitter, tragic thing. "The Army has to fix its blame on the living; not the dead."

The unfairness of it was gall in Portugee's mouth. "But there will be an investigation, won't there?"

A beaten man nodded. "There always is."

"Then I want to be called when it happens. I want to tell what I saw."

Carrington only nodded again, but a flash of gratitude was in his eyes.

Portugee stood and walked to the door. He looked back from the door. Both men suffered, but each's reason was different. He closed the door behind him.

He and Hattie stood at the gate, watching Carrington and the force that accompanied him. It was useless to express his rebellion. Those wives, accompanying the escort, had insisted upon going too. Nothing would change them. Mrs. Grummond was among those women, riding in a springless wagon. It was beginning to snow again. It would be another brutal trip for every one of them.

Carrington stopped the small procession, and Portugee stepped forward and shook hands. "It's been a pleasure to work under you, sir."

Carrington smiled at him. He had recovered some of his resiliency. "I hoped I would see you, Mr. Phillips. I have said my other good-byes."

"Colonel, could I have a moment to speak to Mrs. Grummond?"

"Certainly," Carrington granted.

Portugee moved down the line to her wagon. He took off his glove and extended his hand.

She took it with both hands, and he felt the pressure of them. "I never did say what was in my heart."

He shook his head. She didn't have to put it into words.

"Do you have to go now? A little later when the weather gets better—" He stopped his words. Nothing would change her mind.

"I couldn't stay here a minute longer than I had to," she said.

178

He understood. Fort Phil Kearny had too many bad memories for her and Carrington.

He stepped back and let the procession go. A great number of Fort Kearny's original people had come out to see Carrington leave, and that was open grief on most of the faces.

Hattie took his hand, and he closed on hers hard. The gates swung behind the last vehicle.

"Look at them," she exclaimed.

He frowned at her, not at the moment getting what she meant. Hutson and Kathy stood together, her hand enfolded in his. The thoughts of the colonel would pass quickly for most of all these people. It would be eliminated by the thoughts of a new future that had suddenly been handed to them. It was plain to see where Hutson's and Kathy's were.

"Couldn't you go to the new colonel and ask him now, John?"

His frown didn't leave. This was one he didn't catch at all.

"Oh, John," she said in exasperation. "Can't you see? How much longer do they have to wait?"

"You mean—" If it was what he thought it was, she was asking a lot of him.

"Yes," she snapped. "Who would be better qualified? Doesn't the new colonel owe you something?"

The laughter started, and he couldn't stop it. The indignation in her eyes only increased it. Once a woman got an idea in her head, that she thought was logical, nothing could knock it out.